# DEADLIER THAN THE MALE

P. Nandakumar Warrier

Leadstart
INKSTATE

ISBN 978-81-948044-6-8


First published in India 2020 by Inkstate Books
An imprint of Leadstart Publishing Pvt Ltd

Sales Office:
Unit No.25/26, Building No.A/1,
Near Wadala RTO,
Wadala (East), Mumbai – 400037 India
Phone: +91 969933000
Email: info@leadstartcorp.com
www.leadstartcorp.com



Disclaimer: The views expressed in this book are those of the Author and do not pertain to be held by the Publisher.

Editor: Vaibhav Pathare
Cover: Nitin Ingale
Layouts: Victor Patali

*To... Lionel Aranha,*
*friend and philosopher*

# About the Author

Nandakumar Warrier was educated at Guindy Engineering College, Case Western Reserve University and the University of Stockholm, and has lived for many years in Sweden, the USA, Oman, and New Zealand. His longest stints of work were at the Institute of International Economic Studies (IIES), Stockholm, and the National Institute of Economic Research (Konjunktur Institutet), Stockholm, following which he joined the faculty of the Indian Institute of Management, Kozhikode.

# Acknowledgements

I would like to thank the constantly transforming community at IIM Kozhikode (IIMK), comprising students, faculty members, and staff members, who have provided the raw, exciting material for this novel - with their ambitions, dreams, zest for life, plots and unexpected sacrifices in an atmosphere of intense competition. Cheick Wague from the University of South Stockholm at Södertörn and Bala Batavia of DePaul University Business School, who were frequent visitors at IIMK, provided valuable inputs for the story with their insights and shrewd observations about individual and group interactions at the institute.

I would also like to express my warm appreciation for the invaluable inputs from the Leadstart editorial team, Malini, Devanshi, Pooja, Naina, and my editor Vaibhav. I can now understand how many an unpolished stone has become a sparkling entity by passing through their hands!

My wife Sheela's moral support and ability to provide solutions for intricate problems of all sorts have been crucial for the success of this venture. So have the encouragement from my daughters, Sitara and Nirupama, who have sacrificed our togetherness during extended writing periods.

# Contents

# Author's Note

This is entirely a work of fiction and does not deal with any living people or actual incidents; nor does it depict social relations or administrative and academic practices at any of the brilliantly functioning Indian Institutes of Management.

I

'Madam, the architect is waiting'.

She looked up in irritation. The secretary, Bhaskaran, had entered without knocking. She glared at him. The man shifted uneasily.

'Madam, I am here because he has been waiting for half-an-hour'.

A meek tone now, she could hardly hear him.

'Don't be here for the wrong reasons. I said I'll tell you when I'm ready to see him, didn't I?'

Bhaskaran swallowed rapidly and exited, bowing slightly and moving backwards.

'They'll make mincemeat of you in Kerala', her colleagues at IIMB had told her, gloating. 'Didn't you read about the director of the Centre for Population Studies, Trivandrum, who tried to commit suicide? We wouldn't want to see such a news-report about Prof. Sujata Das, faculty on leave from IIMB'.

Sujata had joined in the general laughter, but had even then, at that point of time itself, decided to prepare the ground carefully before taking up the job as director, IIMK.

And prepare the ground in what sense? Well, in the traditional, time-honoured policies of the rulers of the land, right from the days of Chandragupta Maurya and Kautilya: get information from informers, spies.

Getting information about the state of affairs in other IIMs was not difficult, given the close, albeit informal organizational ties between all these haloed institutions. For instance, one ready source was the interaction between IIM librarians who met several times each year for some reason or other: improving infrastructure, software, data collection, and so on. The IIMK librarian, a habitual drunkard, could be plied with Scotch whisky and made to talk like a trained vocal parrot about all his colleagues, staff and faculty. There were a few other channels of confidential information available to the discerning interlocutor.

'This fellow Bhaskaran would be horrified to know that I have the rundown on all his petty vices', Sujata smiled to herself as she was recollecting the IIMB origins of her strategies.

She had to admit to herself that her IIMB colleagues were right. IIMK was difficult territory–but not in the way they painted it. She knew that she would have to lay down strict honour codes for faculty and students. Faculty members at IIMs were often   prone to excessive flamboyance and sarcasm, considering themselves to be the highest echelons of academics in the country, while students, as self-proclaimed geniuses, somtimes took unwarranted liberties.

Rather surprisingly, perhaps, there weren't any underground Maoist or Naxalite - or even ordinary communist - cells at the institute, despite its location in Kerala. No outsider political leader of labour unions. The workers were often up in arms, but on individual issues, often at loggerheads with each other, and not in a joint confrontation with the management. They somehow seemed to have a sense of pride in belonging to an elite national institute.

Yet, she had the eerie feeling that  the institute was as if on mined grounds.  She was not a socially conservative person but had to concede that there were dangerous undercurrents at work, in areas that could be taboo terrain.

At least two such undercurrents.

First, as to be expected at any campus of higher learning: drugs.

Less common to normal campus life was what her informants told her about a homophobic group at IIM Kozhikode. It had emerged suddenly but had dissipated suddenly too, for no apparent reason, just as had happened with the Klux Klux Klan. Perhaps it had become inactive because its vociferous leader had left to take up another job, but could return to life at any point in time.

For her, all this spelled out a strong possibility of tragedy striking at any point in time at IIMK.

She was surprised that it hadn't happened so far.

II

The architect could wait, no harm done. He had not delivered the goods he was supposed to: something to surpass the Greek pavilion, a part of which she could see from the broad window running the entire length of the wall behind her main writing table.

She had wanted a plan for a high walk-bridge that connected the faculty residence hill with the main hill housing all academic and administrative buildings. A high, generously curving piece of art that would be visible from afar, become a landmark for the entire region.

But this architect buffoon had come with a plan for a small, low-level bridge, rather like a railway platform over-bridge. One look - and she knew it for what it was.

'Is this a bridge over a road or between two hills?'. she had asked without taking a second look.

'Well, it's like this: the faculty members can come down from the residence hill and then use the over-bridge to cross the road towards their offices'.

She snorted in disgust, and had thrown those papers on the table in front of his face, and asked him to return only when he had done what he had been clearly instructed to.

The Greek pavilion was also a fine piece of art, she had to admit. Several pillars with crowns of flowers and leaves. Hard to understand why no one seemed to use the place for what it was supposed to be: a quiet location for meditation. But then that was the sad case with many innovations on campus. The gymnasium, the walkway around the lake with lights all along. She had discontinued the lighting to cut energy costs as no one was using the walkway anyway, not even lovers.

She could see someone moving between the pillars of the pavilion. It was Rakesh, the Strategy area faculty member, and a fresher, a first-year boy. She couldn't recollect the name. Informal counseling obviously, that's good undoubtedly, cannot allocate a faculty member for every student on campus.

She rather liked Rakesh. He had been around, on various short teaching assignments in many countries after his Ph.D. from Toronto, before landing up at IIMK on a permanent job. A quick, alert chap. Swift movements like a bird looking for food scraps. When she had called him over for an informal chat–as she did for every faculty member soon after taking charge- he had pulled out a chair lightning-quick and had virtually hopped on to that. At the introductory session for student interviews, with everyone standing in an enormous hall, she had noted his quick gestures again, moving within the crowd so fast that people had to keep turning their necks to keep track of him. Nothing escaped his attention. At one stage he had pushed out a chair from the sidelines and stood on it to get everybody's attention.

She told herself, these student interviews were good occasions for studying the individual – the faculty member, that is. She made it a point to sit for a fair amount of time with each interviewing faculty group, staying along with them in hotels and guesthouses.

Some incidents that occurred during these straightforward duties were just too raw to believe. At one interview, a faculty member asked the candidate blatantly:

'And what may be your caste?'

He must have forgotten her presence in the interview room. But he was reminded of that at once:

'That's enough, you may leave the room'

She had addressed the–later crestfallen - faculty member, not the student. And this was one fellow who had come to her room soon after her arrival with a detailed presentation which she cut short rudelyon why he needs to be promoted to a professor's post.

Another equally raw incident took place in the 'after-hours', at around nine one interview day evening. There was a knock on the door, and at the door stood a faculty member, Dr. Mishra. Obviously drunk, but does one become blind when drunk? He must have mistaken her for an accompanying female teacher, for he said–while trying to push in past her:

'I'm coming in, have some quality stuff'.

'No, you're not'.

The sound of the resounding slap must have echoed in the corridor. But when she peered around the door after his swaying body, retreating with profuse apologies, she could see no one.

All this goes to show that one can never predict what these fellows can come up with, even though they may seem to follow a stable pattern. This nocturnal raider had become predictable as an interviewer. He would ask every single candidate:

'Put down the Fourier series', extending a pen and a sheet of paper.

Past candidates hasten to help their fellow sufferers, who follow, by posting repeated interview questions on the web. So, the 'Fourier' series question had become famous. Once, a candidate pulled out and extended a pre-written answer, graciously refusing the sheet of paper extended to him by the interviewer.

She could no longer see Rakesh and the fresher boy in the pavilion. Only the dragonflies were to be seen, as always flying around in hordes, sometimes hovering still, helicopter-like. This must have been their territory always intruded upon by IIMK.

Time to finally call the architect. She had a feeling that her hand-drawings of the walk-bridge would make more practical sense too–not just aesthetic sense.

# III

Pale sunlight.

Shades of light green wherever the eye falls.

That's how Divya would always remember the IIMK campus. She was standing with her parents a few weeks after classes had started at the edge of the lawn between buildings when they saw the director at the other end of the green expanse. Her parents had hurried across, pulling her along. She had protested vehemently, not wishing to be noticed by the stern eyes of the 'iron lady', but to no avail.

What she didn't know was that her parents had met Sujata Das even before the term started. They had given her some excuse for their absence; besides, she was to leave herself for spending a few days with her aunt; some other relatives would also be at the aunt's, to celebrate the family girl's admission into a prestigious institution.

Pale sunlight. That would be how her parents would also remember the campus which would give them great pain as well as pleasure. They had walked along the winding path to the director's office, both sides lit up an unusual light green by the sun's rays. When they told the secretary at the director's office how the soothing yellow light appealed to them, he had smiled and said,

'Yes, indeed, we say "Ilam veiyil" for this in Malayalam'.


They hadn't requested an appointment. But Sujata had asked Bhaskaran to let in the couple as she did not expect any complaints before the year began.

She read them at a glance: a middle-aged rural couple; unused to the hustle and bustle of life at IIMs.

And, clearly worried. Must be about leaving their sheltered offspring to the IIM pack, of which they must have heard a tale or two.

So she came straight to the point.

'You wish to talk to me about your son–or is it, daughter?'

'Yes madam', the man spoke. Rajasthani, she guessed. Probably in his early fifties, honest, troubled faced, dressed in an ill-fitting grey safari suit. The Rajasthani rural dress would have passed him better. His wife was in traditional attire, a handsome lady with sharp features and colourful bangles up to her upper arms.

'Madam, Divya is a strong, determined girl, but has been through a crisis. I will be honest; she has tried to take her own life once'.

Sujata said nothing, clasped her hands in front of her face, and sat still, listening.

'He was a boy she used to train field events with. She told us about him, of their plans to get married. Then he...'

A sob from the Rajasthani lady broke the narrative. Her husband looked at her sorrowfully but motioned to her to control herself.

'Then he got a sports scholarship to America and left, promising to come back and take her later. There were some letters, but they stopped coming after a few months. He broke away completely, with no explanation'.

'I can imagine the shock', Sujata said finally, 'too much for a young girl who had placed her trust in someone for the first time. You don't have to go into painful details about her trauma. But why are you telling me this now?'

'Oh madam, so you know.  If the schedule here is too difficult, and she is under great stress……', his voice trailed away.

'Not to worry!'. Sujata got up briskly, signaling dismissal.  'It's not like an IIT with everything hanging around exams day after day. The program includes much more role-plays, group interactions, all of which would bring more stability to the individual student, reduce mental stress. But', she added kindly, 'we will monitor her, you can  rest assured'.


And now they stood, the entire family, in front of her, at the edge of the outdoor auditorium on the lawns. A confident girl, rearing to go, was Sujata's impression once again. That was what she had felt when she had called the girl over on some pretext soon after the first meeting with her anxious parents. Convent-educated, not a rural type like her mother, not scared of anything either, from the looks of her.

'Just wanted to say goodbye', the man said hesitatingly.

Sujata ignored him.

'And how have been your beginning - term classes?

She scrutinized the girl more closely. Smartly turned out, in tight-fitting black pants and a blue shirt. Bobbed hair framing a pretty round face. Alert, but somewhat dreamy, eyes. Taller than what one would expect from her parentage.

For her part, Divya felt nothing but admiration–not even fear–for the woman in front. Steel grey hair, with a firmly set face and a fairly prominent jaw. Though a few inches shorter, it was as if the woman towered over her.

'Rough times in microeconomics and introductory accounting, am I right? I imagine you would have enjoyed organizational behavior with the active playgroups.'

Divya's jaw dropped. How could the director guess exactly what she has been through?

'Yes, madam. Mitra sir has been drilling us thoroughly. I am afraid I goofed up on the derivations he wanted me to do on the board–unfortunately, he had picked me out arbitrarily to do those!  He was mad, asked me to come well- read , and prepared for future sessions.'

She grimaced, but then snapped to attention, remembering whom she stood facing.

Sujata smiled a little condescendingly.  It was good for the students to have a rough first term: kept them on their toes and moulded them to be good stress-takers. In fact, the first term was crammed, loaded with courses, two more than the averages for other terms. This was done deliberately.

'Dr. Jyothi has some out-of-the-ordinary teaching methods, I gather'.

'Indeed, madam. We had a role-play session outside, in fact right here where we are standing now, at the outdoor auditorium. Then also at the Greek pavilion.'

'Disturbing the dragonflies', Sujata said under her breath.

'Excuse me, madam?'

'And I gather you are one of the lucky ones with a single room?'

She had thought about it and gave the girl a single room, rather than a room with a mate who could, perhaps, prevent any depression attacks. She had remembered the experience at the United Nations teaching program hostel, when two girl roommates, great company for each other to begin with, had ended up pulling knives on each other.

'I am so happy, madam, I got this room all to myself. And I have some very friendly neighbours to make up for the lack of in-room -company'.

Sujata nodded and then turned and walked away abruptly, waving a hand at the rural couple who were hanging eagerly on every word of hers.


Divya had not been honest with the director about her hotel stay. The girl next door, a pleasant slow-moving Amazon, was indeed a reassuring presence. But late one night, when Divya had gone out into the lobby to drink from one of the water fountains, she had hurried back to her room. She had seen something of an apparition: from the corridor at the opposite end of the lobby, a girl had come staggering and gone past Divya with glazed eyes, seemingly not seeing her at all.

# IV

It took some time for Diya to get used to the IIMK hostel food, especially the 'Kerala ethnic variety'. Fortunately, some guidance in this matter was not long forthcoming.

One Sunday morning, with all the time in the world, she was staring dubiously at the angry-red chutney served along with the ghee roast dosa, when she heard the reassuring words:

'Don't worry, it's not all that spicy. The colour comes from tomatoes, not from chilly powder'.

The boy appeared in front of her and sat down. Oh, the smart kid, Roshan, from abroad! Never at a loss when attacked by Dr. Mitra in the economics class.

'Deepa, isn't it?'

Divya felt offended. Almost all courses had kicked off with the Profs asking the students to introduce themselves. That's how she knew about Roshan, that he had got into IIMK after a bachelors' degree from a U.S university, she didn't catch the name.

'Divya', she corrected curtly.

'Oh, awfully sorry! I'm very good at faces, but terrible at names. But otherwise, you are registered comprehensively in my books. From magical Rajasthan, am I right?'

Divya softened.

'Great, you have gathered that much.'

'I keep my eyes and ears open"

'I noticed you in particular', Divya said honestly, 'because it struck me as strange that you would come over here from the heartland of MBA programs for  Indian business education.'

Roshan looked as if she had scored a direct hit, a bit at a loss for words. Then he said rather vaguely:

'It's a matter of reaching out for the roots, if I may say so. I didn't want to be in India just as a tourist, wanted to be actively involved either in studies or in running an industry. Is it that odd?', he asked defensively.

'No, no, makes sense to me. And to Kerala and IIMK? You happened to get in only here, I suppose.'

'No, actually I happened to get into both IIMA and C. But my family is originally from here, though I was born in the U.S.  I came back to spend some school years, but that was in Bangalore, and then returned to the U.S for completing the final school years and college'.

He paused as if throwing his mind back, a dosa piece held stationary over the red chutney, and then continued:

'Lucky that an IIM started functioning in Kerala; when I heard that, I had at once started planning to do my business studies here'.

So that explains the lack of a pronounced American

drawl, Divya thought. He has spent a number of his formative years in India.

'I believe it was touch and go', she enlightened him. 'Originally the IIM was to come up in Kochi, and then, for some reason, it was decided to locate it in Kozhikode'.

"That wouldn't have mattered to me, I think. Cochin would have been as good as Calicut to me'.

Then he added as an afterthought:

'But Kozhikode has an advantage over Kochi, to me'.

'How's that?

'You see, a family friend of mine lives here. The daughter of a schoolmate of my mom. We got to know this only after I decided to join. And, the surprise of surprises, within walking distance of IIMK.

'How nice! In one of the houses on the approach road–I mean after our fabulous gate?'

"No, the other side. I can walk to her house from the IIMK back-gate in just seven minutes'.

"Oh, I see. I didn't know people lived that close to our hill;

'You bet they do. Even some IIM faculty members. Her immediate neighbor is one of our faculty, she told me. Didn't know the name.'

'Well, stands to reason, I guess. Being a new campus, faculty residences are only coming up gradually'.

'At any rate, slower than the faculty hiring rate. I believe the previous director went on a hiring spree', Roshan said laughing. 'I overheard our PGP secretary Jose joke once that the director used to stand at the town bus stand–and offer a faculty position to the people getting off buses'.

Divya screamed with laughter and then used a napkin to pick up a couple of dosa pieces that had flown off her mouth. Pleased with her reaction, Roshan got up smiling to get another masala dosa.

'Actually, we know so few of the profs personally yet, she said in a complaining tone. There should have been some formal interaction by now'.

'I think you are better off than me', Roshan said, looking at her archly. 'I see you sometimes jogging along the hill with that strategy Prof.'

'Oh, you mean Rakesh?'

'Is that his name? I see you guys often from the mini football field where I work out'.

'Yeah. I ran into him on my first run downhill. From then on we have coordinated our training'.

'He is on the field too at other times. Dribbles around with one of our classmates, again forget the name. Deepak, I think'.

'Could be. Rakesh is also good at sports medicine, massage, and all that massage and all that'.

'Yes, I could see that. When that fresher – Deepak – fell and hurt himself, Dr. Rakesh gave him a work-over. He was up and dribbling again after ten minutes'.'

Divya nodded, looking impressed.

'Maybe I will join you guys on your run around the lake', Roshan smiled wryly. 'But then three may not add up to good company'.

'But seriously', he continued, 'I think the faculty-student interactions will be formally sparked off by the fresher party that the seniors are throwing for us. Faculty are invited too.'

'You could be right', Divya didn't sound convinced. 'But do you think the profs will come and let their hair down? I believe it is a free-for-all at the IIM parties at the Taj, with liquor flowing and wild dancing'.

'I could imagine someone like your Rajesh, sorry, Rakesh, enjoying the fresher party. But some others wouldn't want to put themselves in compromising positions: how can they act stern and righteous and be taskmasters in the classroom afterwards?'

He cackled and Divya joined in.

They sat silent for a while, in no hurry to leave the dining hall. There was plenty of reading to do, but lazy Sunday mornings are not easily given up. Then, looking out through the glass windows that stretched across all sides of the hall, Divya remarked:

'It's nice that you have a life outside campus. Some of us go to the Taj on the weekends and that's it. No connections at all to the society here. '

'You know, you should tag along when I go to visit my friend Shalini next. She's quite an interesting person'.

'Maybe I will', Diya sounded doubtful.

Finally, they got up to leave. As they were placing their plates on the moving belt, Roshan became more persuasive.

'Really, you should get to know her. Very involved in the local society, just what you seem to yearn for. She conducts dance classes for children as well as tuition in usual school subjects. Free of cost, she has private wealth'.

Then he laughed out. 'And, believe it or not, she even does some matrimonial matching. Didn't want to give up what her dad had been doing, and was known for in this region'.

'I don't know about marriage matching', Divya smiled. 'But helping out school kids is just fantastic. My mom always used to make the girls who came as home help literate. But I guess this may not be as important in 100 % literate Kerala'.

'True. I believe one cannot even get house help here, what with all the - worker- drain to the Gulf Roshan laughed and added: ' and as far as literacy goes, the joke is that Kerala has moved beyond 100% literacy, with a cartoon depicting a monkey sitting on a tea stall chair reading the morning daily Manorama!'

He was pleased again to hear the pearly laugher from this girl he found attractive.  She said now as she turned away:

'Maybe I *will* tag along when you visit our friend, Shalini next time, right?  I think we will have some things in common'.

# V

Sujata was finding it difficult to delegate authority officially–even though she had established several task-specific administrative posts for faculty members. In doing so, she went further than the usual IIM tradition of having only major administrative positions like the PGP, Placement Chairpersons, etc. Still, the most important of all these posts was that of the PGP Chair. In that weighty chair, she had placed Dr. Chari, after a seminar cum interview selection process. To lure him away from IIMA, where he had a family-related locational advantage, she had used the bait of a promotion to associate professor level: real poaching, about which she often gave lectures to corporate audiences.

But belying her expectations, Chari had turned out to be rather weak-willed, unable to take any decisions that would invite criticism or controversy.

'Why does he go around as if on a vow of silence', she asked Jose once. 'I'll give him one term, not more. If he does not match up, I'll dethrone him and load three extra courses on him'.

'Perhaps I adopted too dominant an approach when taking over the IIMK reins', she told herself' may have put the overwhelmingly young faculty group too much on the defensive, afraid to open up on any discussion on key issues'.

'Well, actually the former directors are to blame', she excused herself, following standard strategy: hiring fresh Ph.D.'s who are like hatched chicks taking first steps. The director is then a dictator!'

She felt that this policy of hiring younger faculty members that her predecessors had followed was backfiring. In newly begun institutions, the experienced directors taking charge often adopted such a strategy because young academicians are more pliable, questioning the leadership rarely. Grey-haired faculty members with weighty CVs could sometimes ask nasty questions to put the director in a poor light–which, they may believe, clears their path to the top post. There are even examples in IIMs of senior faculty members collecting signatures to lobby the Human Resources Ministry to dismiss their reigning director.

One unfortunate development with Chari was that she had had to refuse his visit for a term to the Asian Institute of Technology in Bangkok. His selection, on an application forwarded through official government channels, had come through after he was appointed Postgraduate Programme (PGP) Chair. Then, to her as well to as other IIMK staff who interact with the PGP chairperson, it was inconceivable that he could just drop the post like a sack of hot potatoes and take off to Bangkok. Ever since that refusal, he had been going around with a permanent sour expression on his face.

Actually, poor Chari was having a tough time. Not enough faculty to teach elective courses, not enough staff support for the PGP program–only two secretaries when the older IIMs had four or even six.

Chari was given a free hand by the director to bring in visitors, no specific upper limits imposed. To her, there was no choice: getting regular faculty was a time-consuming process. But Chari overplayed his hand:

The student PGP program representatives had asked for and finally got an appointment with the director. A very urgent matter, they had stressed when requesting the meeting. Sujata gave them fifteen minutes.

'Madam,' the student representative Elizabeth leaned forward with an intense expression on her face, 'the consumer behavior course is just going nowhere'.

'Make yourself clear. Going nowhere? What is that supposed to mean?'

Elizabeth swallowed nervously but continued.

'Beg your pardon madam, what we mean is that it is all loose ends, not a…a coherent whole. And the reason is that there are too many teachers'

'Too many? At the same time, in the same class?'

Again, Elizabeth gulped. This was becoming more difficult than the student thought when she took the initiative on what she thought was a worthwhile struggle, for the good of the senior batch.

'No no, sorry madam, what I mean to say is that the course is handled by three separate teachers. They come in for brief periods, sometimes for just three lectures. Before the topic they had handled is completed the next one of the three flies in to give three lectures on a different topic.'

The girl looked anxiously at Sujata's face to see how

she was taking it. Something seemed to reassure her, and she continued:

'We feel that everything differs too much between the approaches of the three teachers. Their teaching style, evaluation, can see that even from the mid-term exams and results. You can get an A-grade result for one of the teachers and an F-level result for one of the others.

She placed her hand on her chest, oath-taking style. 'This has happened to me personally, madam!'

Sujata listened to the student without cutting her short, even though she thought the girl had begun to ramble now– the complaint about inconsistent grading was plain bullshit. But there was something seriously wrong with the way the course had been designed. This was news to her. Though individual course organization was PGP Chairperson's territory, she scolded herself for having failed to observe such a pronounced transgression of the course norms. If she had been aware of such goings-on, she would have acted immediately to correct the anomaly. Visits by outside faculty were unavoidable given the shortage of internal faculty, but that didn't mean an avalanche of visitors was to be permitted.

Sujata now nodded at the student as if to tell her it was a good initiative on her part to try to save the course.

'All this sounds odd. But, of course, the PGP Chairman may have some sound reason for having organized the course in this manner. It could be also that he has laid out the second half of the course in a more traditional way. '

She again nodded at Elizabeth, this time in dismissal.

But the students hung on, wanting to make the best of

the opportunity of a face-to-face meeting with the director they had contrived to get.

'If we could take just one more minute of your time, madam,' the sole boy in the representative team of three leaned forward, almost falling out of his chair, 'students are also having difficulty in attending classes organized outside the campus by one of these three teachers'.

'Outside campus?', Sujata said, surprised. IIMK conducted classes at the regional engineering college premises, but that was before the new campus came upon the hills of Kunnamangalam.

Encouraged by having sprung a surprise on the director, the bespectacled boy continued eagerly:

'Yes, madam, at the Taj, in the lobby, sometimes even in the garden. Usually as late as 11 P.M. Mr. Jha has done this on all his visits so far. Says he has to do so as he has to take a flight early next morning'.

Frankly, madam', Elizabeth interrupted the boy, 'students have not been impressed with Mr. Jha. Why he comes for lectures carrying an A-4 sized tray filed with papers. Carries the tray everywhere, even to the canteen, we have never seen him take any papers from that! Some students say it is all show and nothing else!'.

Sujata became stern. This was really in poor taste from the students. How that visitor walks around is nobody else's business. At this rate, the kids will giggle behind her back if she walks holding her head slanted to one side.

'You can't blame or make fun of someone for the way he carries around; Up to him or her to use an executive briefcase, A-4 tray, or a sack.'

The students looked embarrassed, as if they had been caught with their pants down. They looked at each other as if to ask whose idea was it to bring up this stupid point.

'On the other hand, having midnight classes and using exotic locations raises some serious issues. I'll speak to the PGP Chairman'.


Chari must have got wind of the move by the students, bypassing his authority, for he appeared in front of Bhaskaran's desk as soon as the student delegation had trooped out. Sujata noticed his prompt appearance but kept him waiting for a long while to sweat him out.

When the PGP Chairperson was finally ushered in, Sujata gave him a cold stare and motioned to the seat in front of her oval-shaped desk. Then she turned her attention to the paper in front of her and started writing. Chari sat at the edge of the chair, fidgeting.

'What's the story on three visitors for the Consumer Behaviour course? More than a dozen return air tickets from Ahmedabad! Or is it fifteen? I could have brought the chairman of the Harvard marketing department for this cost.'

She continued to write, which made Chari even more nervous.

'Of course, Madam, it is expensive. I will be the first to point that out. But Consumer Behaviour is a key elective. Students will revolt if that is scrapped.'

'Not good enough. You should have asked one of the visitors to stay for half a course period at least. Four visits each for three visitors! Utter nonsense.'

Chari spluttered, said something to the effect it will not happen again. But he was not to be let off so easily.

'And what's all this about classes in the Taj lobby? Perhaps at the bar too, I presume.'

Chari looked shocked. He hadn't thought such course-specific day-to-day information will reach the eyes of the director.

'Mr. Agarwal was pressed for time, I gathered, 'he said in a pleading tone. 'He organized that class the night before his departure.'

'And Taj is part of the IIMK classroom blocks, is that so?'

Chari said nothing, looked down, biting his nails.


Sujata told herself to behave. After all, she was speaking with the PGP Chair, the highest administrative post at the institute after the director. The low median age of the faculty members at the institute should not make her fall into a pattern of being too dominant in personal interactions. It was just that, as Chari had realized with a shock, she had been receiving too much disturbing news about the way the PGP program was functioning.

This fellow Chari didn't know that she was getting detailed inputs on all matters – particularly the conflicts–relating to the PGP Program from Jose, one of the PGP secretaries. Jose was at IIMB before he transferred to IIMK, and she had been on very good terms with him there. He had come back after his IIMK interview, held barely a week after the institute started functioning, and confessed to her that that was the first time he had been north of Trichur in his home state. In this he was like the foreign tourists who travel north in Kerala from the famed Kovalam beach: first to Kochi to see the Jewish synagogue and the Chinese fishing nets, and then up to Trichur to see the Pooram festival where two hundred elephants stand side by side swaying to drum beats. But not further, rarely to Calicut. So, they give a miss to Calicut with its rich history, beaches, mountains, forests just an hour and a half away, and a tradition of hospitality and warmth towards strangers.

'I felt ashamed when one of the interview panel members asked me if I have been to Calicut before', Jose told her screwing up his face. 'That lady looked astounded when I told her no, unfortunately never before'.

She now threw out a piece of information that added to Chari's woes; again, concerning the midnight 'lobbyist'.

'You are no doubt aware that Mr. Agarwal is one of the largest tax-debtors, that is, with unpaid due taxes to the Government of India'.

Chari was sweating even in the air-conditioned room.

'But Sujata madam, I had no idea at all…..'

'As the PGP Chair, you are expected to check the background and credentials of the visitors to whom you send invitations.  They have to be checked very thoroughly, with no room for error. In the case of the regular faculty hired, that task falls to me–and I can assure you that there has been no shortcoming in that respect'.

'But are you sure madam…'

Sujata just waved him away, looking down at her papers. The man got the message and got up to leave, but could exit only after another barrage of scathing words:

'Please make sure Dr. Chari that the visitor's program is cleaned up and run efficiently, with no margin for unpleasant incidents. It is the very reputation of the institute that is at stake, I think you'll agree with me'.

After Chari left, she sat pondering over a couple of other matters that Jose had brought up to her attention. He must have felt they were important issues: otherwise, he would not have bypassed the PGP Chairman and come straight to her. Of course, he mentioned other minor matters to her, most of which deserved only laughter tinged with sarcasm—such as the PGP Chairman's outbursts.

Jose had rushed once to Dr. Chari's room, hearing him screaming and had taken in the situation at a glance. Chari was dealing with a girl student who had been caught copying in an exam and was getting her to write an apology and an acceptance of the punishment of a drop in grade by one unit—such as from A to B. That was when the girl's friend, boyfriend to be more precise, entered without permission and started arguing in her favour.

And that was when Jose heard Chari scream:

'How dare you! You write a letter of apology too, or it is a grade reduction for you too!'

Jose had soothed Chari's ruffled feathers and pushed the boyfriend firmly out of the room. The boy went without further protest—for he didn't want a grade cut.

While there were many such minor irritants in the functioning of the program, they didn't require Sujata's intervention. However, more serious issues reared their heads once in a while and were not amenable to solution by solo action from the PGP Chairperson.

One such issue was the relationship between various departments, especially those that straddled both academics and administration. Placement or even a pre-placement period program under the auspices of the faculty and the student placement chairpersons often clashed with the PGP program, with dual bookings of classrooms. Thus, conflicts between these two departments became rampant during specific periods.

One day, when Dr. Salim entered the class for his course in fundamentals of corporate finance, he thought that he saw strange faces. This basic course in finance is taken by first-year students, but looking at him with surprised expressions were final year students. One of them gasped:

'Oh, Prof. Salim, we are having a pre-placement session here'.

'How can that be', Salim flared up, 'this classroom is reserved in advance for my finance course?

Just then the placement chairperson Sangeeta entered the room.

'Sorry, Dr. Salim. This lecture hall has been booked for me'.

'By whom, would you be kind enough to tell me?'

And so, it went on, more people entering the fray, and, accordingly, several versions reached Sujata's ears. The strange part was that there was no shortage of classrooms. Of course, some were better-located, with fantastic views over the hills and so on. The facts of the matter were difficult to disentangle from the different reports, but Sujata concluded that bad blood between the second PGP secretary Shankaran and the placement secretary, as well as between the respective student representatives had led to the conflict situation.

The interdepartmental conflicts even spilled over into discussions of social etiquette. Some senior students complained that the PGP secretary Shankaran had demanded that he be addressed as 'sir'–and not as 'plain Shankaran'. Such a demand contrasted starkly with the wish of some faculty members to be on a first-name basis with their students.

While all this sounded quite silly, it gave strength to Sujata's conviction that all the faculty and staff should be given some training in social etiquette; after all, the selected Indian Administrative officers, of both the IAS and the IFS cadres, go through such training. She had also observed the very specific ways in which government officials of some western nations toast when taking a drink, lifting the glass and nodding to each other both before and after taking a sip.

There was a controversy within the placement section itself. The CEO of a leading consultancy firm had backed out from his agreement to take part in the placement program after receiving the following message from a placement student representative:

'Hi, there! How are things? So when are you landing up here at good old IIM Kozhikode?'

Clearly, this student could have benefitted from some training in social etiquette.

Pressing through all these matters were, requiring

short-term as well as long-term measures, what was most disturbing to Sujata was the breach in accepted codes of faculty-student relationships. What occurred between teacher and student after the latter left IIMK belonged to private territory: was a personal matter. A student and his or her ex-professor may engage in any kind of personal relationship, moral or immoral, extra-marital, or anti-social. All this may not set good precedents in a harmonious society, but that was not IIMK business.

However, while they were still part of the IIMK fraternity, faculty and students had to follow certain–albeit unwritten–norms. No favoritism by any teacher towards any student, no sexual relations - as the faculty-student relationship is one of dependency and wielding of authority.

It was therefore understandable that Sujata took the information about the violations of the well-defined limits in the relationship between students and faculty members seriously. Jose had waited quite a while, had noted repeated instances of favouritism before going to the director with 'soundproof'. He did not approach Chari before the meeting with the director, for he felt that Chari will be unwilling, even scared to talk with the concerned faculty member.

In one case, perhaps the most straightforward and directly observable of all the 'favouritism' episodes, a faculty member allowed a student to register for his course very late, after the mid-term examination. The girl student involved had made some tentative approaches to Jose about late registration, receiving a firm 'no'. Then she had gone to the teacher himself. A good-looking girl, not averse to showing off her attractive physical attributes.

And, presto, the professor agreed. The student ended

up with an A-minus for the course. To be fair to her, she was a bright student with a good grade point average. But it has to be added that–though this did not become the talk of the town at IIMK–the student and theprofessor were seen together often at the Taj. And then not just at the restaurant and the bar, but even in the elevators going jump to the rooms and suites.

In some other cases, favouritism was nailed, confirmed by Jose only after repeated observations. He found some faculty members closing their eyes to repeated absenteeism – that  would push down attendance below required levels – and to instances of copying in examinations and reproduction of earlier term papers written by previous batch students.

'What, Dr. Rakesh too? I find it hard to believe!'

Sujata was upset about this negative observation about a favourite of hers but decided not to take any immediate action. She wanted to first find out the underlying reason for such an act of favouritism on his part. A nagging doubt clawed at her when she recalled some information she had received from 'informers' about the dangerous flashpoints at IIMK.

The other act of favoritism noted by Jose was from a faculty member who had joined IIMK from IIT Kharagpur. Jose had already registered his name mentally for making irresponsible statements like:

'Junkies and boozers are the best! Always trustworthy!'

But whereas Dr. Rakesh seemed to shower his favouritism on freshman year males, the IIT prof. made no such discrimination, favouring both selected boys and girls–obviously the ones that are trustworthy in his view!

These reports from Jose disturbed Sujata profoundly. She realized that she had been resting on her oars, after some preliminary research on IIMK social equations and dynamics. Now it struck her that these dangerous currents could take the institute to the brink of a great chasm unless some strong intervention was forthcoming from the institute leadership: from her.

# VI

Divya took the route she had taken a few times earlier, cutting through behind the computer building, on the side with the huge beehive up on top. IIMK students and staff usually avoided this side, the giant beehive serving as a deterrent. But the isolated grassland below the hive was pretty, studded with wild yellow and pink flowers.

But on the usually isolated sloping grassland, she saw a small group. A food delivery boy, the well-known hotel's sign displayed on his box, was handing over some packets. In fact, she had come across the same group in the same place once before. They had noticed her too but had turned their backs to her.

This time they stared at her, not very friendly looks.

No hands raised in greeting.

Today, the girl with the hypnotized look she had run into late one night was there too. It came as a shock to her, set off a chain of wild thoughts.

Was it food delivery or something else?

Drugs?

This delivery man was a ubiquitous presence, to be seen all over campus. Why here, under the forbidding beehive?

She went through the back-gate and after a brisk walk, turned into the side-road leading eventually to Shalini teacher's house. She stopped short as she saw a couple of strangers lounging against a wall a bit further down the path. She had never come across anyone, barring some typical local people in traditional dress on that village road.

The men moved slowly to the middle of the path as she started moving forward again.

To her, it felt like a threatening move, a blatant warning to keep off.

Then, hearing the sound of a motorbike, she turned around. It was the food delivery man taking a fast turn into the narrow path. She could hear her heart begin to pound.

# VII

One Sunday afternoon, she had finally fallen in step with Roshan when he was off for the usual sojourn with his family friend.

'You seem to have found a soul-mate', she said, noticing the spring in his step.

'You could say that', Roshan laughed. 'But it may well be a one-way street. She may be just tolerating me as I am a family friend. A necessary evil! However,' he added, straightening his shoulders, 'I don't think so. I believe she looks forward to my visit'.

Diya decided to pull his legs a bit. 'I remember you saying that she runs a marriage agency too, besides giving free classes to schoolchildren. Maybe she could find a bride for you.'

Roshan stopped and looked at her in genuine surprise.

'What, Divya, are you a mind-reader or something? I have already told her to keep a lookout for me. Coming back to my roots, as I told you once before.'

'You must be kidding!'

'Not at all. You know, Indian girls in the U.S would rather not marry Indians straight off the hotplate from India : what if the boy expects them to do all the housework, starting with serving the morning coffee?  It scares them. But with Indian- American boys, even born and brought up in the U.S, it is often the other way around. They would love to marry girls from India.

'Straight off the hot plate, eh? So she would do all the housework, bring him coffee at break of dawn'.

'No, no, you are missing the point. It's just that they feel that girls from India will be more family-oriented, stay loyal to their men, not breaking up the marriage for a silly reason, and so on.'

He threw a sideways glance at Divya.  'Why, I know of a couple in the U.S that got divorced because they could not decide who would vacuum clean which day of the week!'

'That, anyway, I won't believe', Divya said smiling. 'But I see your point. You belong to that group of optimistic Indian Americans with a solid trust in tradition.'

The walk was turning out to be longer than what Roshan had indicated. First close to fifteen minutes along the main road at the back of the Institute, then into a narrow road to the right, and then they had been walking for another ten minutes.

'Soon now; a turn to the right, and then we are there', Roshan assured her. 'I got lost the first time I went to Shalini's place. The local people have such an odd way of giving directions. "Go west, then turn south, head east for a while, and then take the third turn to the north".  How could I ever find her house with such instructions! I had no idea, in an unfamiliar place, which is west, north, and south.'

'No street signs or housing colony signs either, can't see any', Divya concurred.

'You bet. No signs at all. Why I have seen perfect street signs on glaciers and underground locations'.

'On glaciers? Under the earth! Roshan, you are talking gibberish'.

'Sorry, not glaciers. I got carried away. But I'm not exaggerating all that much. Once, only once, I got selected for a student exchange program, and then to an unusual location. To the extreme north of Sweden, to the cities of Lulea and Kiruna.  Ultima Thule, one can say. The Lulea river gets frozen in winter, and becomes a playground for cars and skaters. There are then signs on the frozen river giving directions - to streets, places, restaurants, and so on.

'Wow, unbelievable!'

And, in Kiruna, which has one of the world's largest iron ore mine, highways are adding up to some 64km highways of a total length of 64 km, with street-signs and speed limits'.

Divya seemed to be struck dumb.

'But, sadly, the mine poses a threat to the very city of Kiruna itself. It is caving in towards the city. So, the town has to be evacuated in twenty years or so. But am I boring you?'

'No, you have been around a lot, Roshan. And so, you will naturally have many tales to tell, I can imagine'.

'Then let me tell you another tale since I am on this

top gear anyway', Roshan laughed. In that same northern region, I went on a sightseeing trip to a hill. Not an ordinary hill, though it seemed innocent enough. In the Cold War decades, it was a bastion, a solid area of defense against any invasion from the east. A wooded hill, but the top of the hill could open for helicopters and aircrafts. The front of the hill could open up for vehicles and tanks. There were also street-signs and directions to hospitals, dispensaries, stores, living areas, etc., inside the hill'.

Divya was getting a bit tired of these Nordic tales, so she tactfully changed the subject.

'You said that Shalini does not charge tuition fees for any of her classes. I guess she must be a wealthy person.'

"That's right. She is quite well off, inherited wealth. But she charges for her occasional dress-making. She is a skillful tailor, a high—end fashion dressmaker'.

'That's awesome!'

'Yep. I believe getting a good tailor is very difficult here. The joke is that you need ministerial influence–like the one about 'coconut-pluckers', that rich businessmen are seeking such men as bridegrooms for their daughters because that is the only way to get this service!'

'Come lay off now!'

The sky had been overcast for quite a while. Now heavy drops of rain had started to fall. A real downpour seemed to be imminent, and they had no umbrellas.

'Just like the day I visited Shalini for the first time', Roshan said while throwing a handkerchief over his head. 'But I reached her house before the rain started lashingdown. No problem now either, we will be there soon'.

When they reached the gate of Shalini's house, Divya liked the place at once. 'A feeling of tranquility', is the way she would have expressed it. A small path with blooming flowering plants on either side led up to the front door, passing by a huge mango tree that stood close to the compound wall. It was a fairly large compound, perhaps twenty cents or more, she guessed. An old house, but done up well, with tiled roofs and traditional windows with no diagonally crossing bars stood away from the road, close to backside wall.

The door opened as soon as Roshan rang the bell. Shaline stood there with a welcoming smile, looking with curiosity at the young girl in front of her. She was younger than Divya had expected, perhaps not more than five years older than Roshan. Luxurious jet-black hair, tied behind in a broad cascading fall in the old Kerala style.

'Divya, I have heard a lot about you', Shalini took her hand, leading her inside into the living room of the house. It was a fairly small room, with sofas made of cane, but a solid teak table in the centre of the room. The table clearly belonged to that earlier era, but the cane chairs seemed to be a modern addition. On the hall hung some black and white family photos and also a couple of Ravi Varma paintings. Roshan saw Divya looking at the paintings, and said 'genuine originals' as he flung himself into the sole easy-chair, also of cane as if that was reserved for him and him only. Shalini took Divya to one of the long three-seater cane sofas and sat in the far corner of the sofa herself.

'Built in the traditional Kerala style', Roshan said, indicating the corridor leading to the inside of the house. Divya nodded; from where she sat, she could see a central square with an open-top, with several rooms on all sides. The small office room attached to the living room may have been, again, a modern addition, she guessed.

'Divya has heard a lot about you too', Roshan remarked to the host. 'So, no need, I presume, for any introductions'.

'It's just so fantastic that you are helping kids in the early development years', Divya said, turning sideways to look earnestly at Shalini. She gazed at the soft, but determined face, the most remarkable feature being the eyes: like deep lakes, but full of life, long eyelashes providing a lovely canopy.

'I was telling Roshan what my mom always did, making sure that every girl who came as house-help left the job fully literate'.

'The kids who come here all attend school', Shalini clarified, 'but almost all of them have weaknesses in one or more subjects. I teach them mainly math and science subjects'.

'I don't know how much help I can be', Divya said hesitatingly, 'but I can be here sometimes, try to help out'.

'That would really be a welcome move'. There was genuine enthusiasm in Shalini's voice. Roshan thought that perhaps she was also eager just for the plain company, of a person like Divya to whom she seemed to have taken to at first sight. 'Feel free to drop in any time. This could be a stress-reduction oasis for you away from IIM's boiling pots! You can even stay over during weekends if you like, there's plenty of room here'. Shalini waved her hands around in an expansive manner.

'Provided she doesn't run into IIM Profs here too',

Roshan struck a cautioning note. 'Didn't you say that you have a neighbor who is an IIM professor? Didn't know his name, though, you had added'.

'Oh yes. I have only two neighbours. The one to the back is a family that has lived there from generations, from Jambavan's time, as we say here in Kerala. Only an old couple left in that sprawling house now; kids and grandchildren are spread out across the globe. The other neighbor, to the right as you can see through that window, is one of your folks'.

'Haven't, you met him? Even in passing?'

'No, never. He moved in a year ago, coming from outside the state, I was told: by the postman who carries information in this locality from house to house. He is known as 'ACV news', the regional news channel by the people around here!'.

Shalini burst out laughing, throwing out her hands and shaking from side to side to Divya's surprise, but rapidly regained her composure and sat still with hands on her lap as if she had been always calm and collected. Divya smiled to herself: so, there are different sides to her newly acquired friend's character!

Roshan had also laughed out, but now probed further:

'So, he knows that faculty member of ours, this postman of yours?'

'Yes and no. Not personally, at any rate. But he has collected information about him, mostly from the part-time cook at that house who is there for only a couple of hours in the forenoon; told me that he is a bachelor, rarely home, so that his incoming post is left outside on the veranda. He also seems to be helping out orphanage children, offers kids meals, toys, etc. May be true; I have seen a foreigner also there with kids, didn't seem to be his own, possibly adopted Indian children'.

'Well, I'm sure we will get to know him soon', Roshan said, looking at the house again through the window. 'As you know, we have only joined recently, and are yet to meet all the faculty members'.

'There are other IIM professors also living around here. But none close by. Three or four of them, I believe'.

'According to ACV News, right!', Divya interrupted. Shalini leaned over and patted her hand, laughing.

'Along with their families. Why is there a shortage of housing at IIMK? With your vast campus; one hundred acres, isn't it?'

'Seems so', Roshan told her. '100 acres, all right, but much of it is on hill slopes. The most beautiful IIM campus, but with a shortage of flat land, not even enough to have a regular football field. We only have a min-football field. And, Divya, who is a sports-enthusiast, and others like Dr. Rakesh, her companion-in-arms, so to say, are the most affected'. Roshan darted a glance at Divya as if to see how she was reacting to the comment.

'Oh, don't exaggerate now', she responded, 'where's the time for any intense sports activities, anyway. Not enough interest either among the students as far as I could see, for any group sports engagements'.

'I'm not exaggerating', Roshan protested. 'No full-fledged football field means no regular 400 meters track to train your middle-distance sprints as you used to do back home at college and school'.

'Something in that I suppose, but it's not the end of the world'. Divya shrugged her shoulders. 'Anyhow, I am here for an MBA, not to train for the Nationals: then I should be at some Sports Authority of India institution'. She looked earnestly at their host. 'The experience I can get here with Shalini will be worth much more than all the athletic training that I will miss'.

The rain had picked up in earnest outside. The sight of the water streaming down the tiled roofs was a novelty to Divya, and she gazed at it with fascination. The rhythmic beat of the water on the roof was also doing wonders for her senses, but when the whole house seemed to shake with a terrific burst of thunder, she instinctively threw her arms around Shalini, who held her, smiling.

'Wait till the rain subsides', Shalini said, 'with such a downpour, you will be soaked even with umbrellas', She, then went and brought hot tea and a plate of Calicut banana and jackfruit chips. 'Next time I can offer you Calicut Halwa. I'm out of it now, and it has to be fresh always'.

They sat there saying nothing much, listening to the patter of the rain on the roof. Divya started going through some family albums that were lying on the table. It was easy to make out Shalini even as a five or six-year-old: the same round, innocent face, large limpid eyes. Engrossed in the pictures, many of them a throwback to the black and white age, she didn't notice her companions leave the room. After a while when she looked up, she saw them in the adjacent office room, looking at a computer screen. The matrimonial-matching efforts, she guessed, giggling, but said nothing. What a way to go, she thought, trying to leapfrog from one world to another without preparation or premeditation. But he might make it all the same, being such a determinedand goal-oriented guy.

Shalini had promised Calicut Halwa the next time. And there were many 'next times' for Divya in the coming weeks. Sometimes she and Roshan visited together, but more often than not, Divya went by herself. Though she did not directly help out with teaching the kids, Shalini had a sense of relief when she was around. It was only during the dance classes that Divya helped out directly, tapping the rhythm to which the children danced. Though she visited every weekend, she never stayed over for the night, for the load of the IIM coursework decreed that she put in a burst of work either late at night or early in the morning; she could not skip both.

..........................................................................................................

As she turned around at the sound of the motorbike and saw the food delivery man speeding towards her, she felt trapped. The strangers, obviously with no good intentions, stood blocking her path forward.

But when she looked back again, the strange men had disappeared, perhaps across the hedges on the sides of the path.

The bike slowed down, the man throwing a searching look at her, then picked up momentum and sped away out of sight. No greeting again from him, though he must have seen her a few times on campus.

She realized her heart was beating wildly, but continued to walk ahead briskly.

Perhaps it was just the stress of the program getting to her. How is she going to manage when the going becomes tough? On the other hand, she had also heard professors say that the final year, at least the final term, is a cakewalk.

Should she share her uneasiness with Roshan? Perhaps not. He may insist that he accompanies her on all her visits to the dance teacher.

# VIII

'Madam, will you be attending the 'freshers' party at the Taj? ', Jose asked at the end of a briefing Sujata had given him.

'You mean the traditional party thrown by the Final Years for the newcomers? Isn't it a little late in the day for that? I believe it is usually held soon after the first term begins'.

'I think the delay is because of some faculty members dragging their feet. Most of them will attend, but it is difficult to get a date to satisfy all of them'.

'Why ask them at all for dates? It is a student affair. Anyway, I am not concerned, won't be attending'.

Sujata looked at Jose with a hint of a smile. 'Also, the students will be happier if the director is not around as a constraining presence'.

Jose smiled back. 'Not necessarily, madam. Former directors have attended the Fresher party and mixed well with the students. Mixed too well, I may add in confidence. One of them had a bit too much to drink and had to be tactfully taken out'.

'Of course, alcohol is served at this party, being a student affair at a private place, not the IIM. But as you are aware, Jose, IIM employees cannot offer alcohol to visitors to IIM, even at private restaurants. Not if it is a formal function. That rule has not been broken here, has it?'

'No madam, that rule has been followed here. The PGP Chairperson never offers alcohol to the visitors taken out using his entertainment allowance. But I have heard stories about other IIMs, not verified, that they violate the rule by putting the item as orange juice on the bill!'.

Jose hid a smile and looked anxiously at the director to see if he had offended her. She was, indeed, not pleased about Jose's revelation, and became formal.

'As I said, I will not be there. But I want you to be there to keep an eye on the boys; and the girls; and the faculty members. I have heard some disturbing things about things that go on; not necessarily at the party, but as its aftermath'.

Sujata fixed a hard stare on the PGP secretary. 'Cannot have the IIM name tarnished in the city. I have heard that the Calicut residents were very proud to get an IIM in their city'.

'Certainly madam, I will be watchful, very alert'.

Then he added as an afterthought:

'Sober too'.

Hearing this solemn promise with an unintended bit of humour, Sujata could not help smiling again. The meeting broke up on this relaxed note.

Perhaps Jose didn't think it was that important, but he

had omitted to mention to Sujata that a girl had been ousted from campus housing because she was found unconscious and drunk in a student corridor. She was allowed to continue the program–but not to live on campus. What Jose didn't know was that Sujata had heard this news, thanks to the generous ranting of her librarian–after a few pegs - at inter-IIM librarian conferences. She also knew that this had happened on the night of a 'Fresher' party; obviously, the party had continued after the students returned to campus.

In her mind, there was also a heavy question mark regarding the reason for the girl student's collapse. Was it alcohol–or something more lethal? Strangely enough, no thorough-going medical examination seems to have been done. The girl was admitted to the campus infirmary and asked leave campus when she had recovered sufficiently.

She looked at her watch. A report to the Human Resources Ministry was due, and she needed a few hours for that. But another appointment had to be attended to, though she had the veto to cancel it: with the campus computer systems manager and head, Mohan. She was a bit intrigued that he had asked for a personal appointment. His work that required her approval was usually discussed at the Systems Committee meeting, of which she was the chairperson and he the executive secretary. Then why had he asked for the meeting today? To ask for a raise? Perhaps to request his elevation to the level of an academic associate professor, as had been done for the librarian–who was his close friend, the two a Laurel and Hardy pair, always together. However, the librarian was able to press his claim through only after taking a Ph.D. in library science, after decades of pursuing that elusive dream.

She didn't like the systems manager, who was a man of few words, but aggressive in getting his demand pushed through. The computer center was located in the massive library building. Originally having to subsist only on a couple of rooms, Mohan had extended his territory over a large chunk of the building. He had achieved this with the connivance of the librarian, whom he had fully under his thumb. The earlier directors had raised no objections because they were too busy expanding teaching and administrative facilities and constructing new blocks.

He had first usurped the third floor of the library building, for setting up a computer lab. However, every IIM student had at least one laptop handy, so the lab was never used by them. They entered the lab only once, at the time of its inauguration. Then it lay empty, at least for its intended activity as far as the students were concerned, with a huge sign of warning posted on the right-hand side glass window: "Do not open, Beehive outside". Definitely a required warning, for a small part of the gigantic beehive was enough to cover the whole glass window.

However, when outsiders - usually school students - were being shown around the campus, they were taken to the lab, and the systems were explained to them. This was done by the Mohan-Sekhar duo sitting now in front of the director, with the help of some research associates.

Later, before the arrival of Sujata on campus, Mohan took over the top floor of the library building also, christening it the 'systems development centre'. Again, it lay empty and unused, OMIT THIS !     since the faculty members were keen only on using the regular library facilities giving them access to journals, books, and magazines.

Sujata had no objection to the use of the IIM infrastructure for public education objectives. Hence, it was with some satisfaction that she sometimes noticed convent school nuns strolling in the Greek pavilion and children disappearing as little dots into the massive library building. These school visits were usually organized on the weekends by the computer systems manager himself.

But while such visits were green-signaled by Sujata, as also by the earlier directors, she put her foot down when the intended use of the facilities by outsiders was film shooting or other kinds of entertainment. Renting out for film production would generate huge incomes, but Sujata will have none of it. In vain, the personnel director, Mr. Kurup, tried to persuade her by saying that the last film shot on campus was a great commercial success.

'What will they project the IIMK campus as, the palatial residence of the chief villain?', she asked sarcastically when a request for filming on campus was made.

But Mohan could carry on with his public education activities without getting clearance on each occasion from the director. In fact, as Sujata had laid mark too, he seemed to avoid having any interaction with her at all–unless necessary, such as when attending the Systems Committee meetings. That was the reason why Sujata was somewhat anxious to know what Mohan had in mind and asked for him to be let into her room immediately.

But she was surprised and rather angry when she saw Sekhar, a faculty member in the Operations Management area, also stepping in diffidently behind the systems manager. She gave him a questioning look which made him slip more behind Mohan. On the other hand, as she had already observed, the computer manager did not flinch before her.

'He's a tough egg', Sujata said to herself, 'despite his well-doer image, there is something fishy about him, I feel it in my bones'.

Resolved to cut the meeting short the moment she found it unworthy of her time, she indicated that they could take their seats.

Mohan took the chair directly opposite her and sat with an expressionless face - a benign round face, befitting his short, plump stature, but belied by small, cold, and watchful eyes. Sekhar, a tall, ungainly man in his early forties, was dressed informally in jeans and a bright t-shirt. Sujata let her eyes run over his dress slowly, expressing her disapproval of such attire for faculty members. She had made this dislike public once, and Sekhar, remembering that, shrunk into his chair.

'You excuse, Dr.Sujata', Mohan said without sounding apologetic at all.

Sujata had noted earlier that he didn't like to call her 'madam', perhaps did not want to let her assume a position of absolute superiority. While he was a superb systems analyst, his English language abilities were very limited– which was rather surprising as his first degree was a B.A in English from some university in the north. He had tried to establish a non-English speaking relation with her, but she had scotched the attempt at the outset itself.

'Dr. Sekhar also has to say to you on the matter I am bringing you. So, I have him with me. Hope you no mind'.

While Sujata was not pleased about the unannounced

addition at the meeting, she was curious to know what the systems manager had in mind. So she nodded almost imperceptibly as a signal to the man to continue.

Now it was Sekhar who spoke:

'It's just that, madam, that since the fresher's party is planned for next week, we thought you should be informed of some unpleasant incidents in connection with that'.

'Unpleasant? Kindly explain yourself'.

Now Mohan took charge but was rather incoherent.

'Bad incident with a girl last year'.

Sujata cut him short. 'Is that all? I have heard about the girl who fainted after the party. Are you here wasting my time repeating that story?'

'No, No', Sekhar started saying, clearly very agitated. Mohan motioned to him to control himself.

'That's the point, Dr. Das, not just drunk', Sekhar said in a calmer tone. 'She was on 'higher ground', as they put it. That is, under the influence of drugs'.

Sujata sat up very straight in her seat. She looked from one to the other and then fixed her eyes unwaveringly on Mohan.

'Drugs?', she said slowly. 'That is a huge allegation. Do you have any proof of what you are saying? Anything at all to support such an insinuation?'

The two men looked at each other as if debating silently on what they should say, what kind of proof to put forward. Then it was Mohan who spoke.

'You right, Dr. Das. No solid proof. But we see things. Here and there'.

'Things? Here and there? '

Sujata could not control her anger. This systems analyst is an intelligent man, she knew very well, notwithstanding his lack of fluency in English. And he sits there now blabbering!

'What he means is, madam', Sekhar cut in, uncharacteristically for him, 'is that students seem to be getting drugs supplied to them from outside'.

Sujata sat up very straight in her seat. A strange look came into her eyes.

'Delivered secretly? At night, you mean? But our security guards work round the clock,no one can enter unobserved.  They always man the gates '.

'No, not only at night, Dr. Das', Mohan said. 'Daytime as well. As food packets, I think'.

Sujata leaned back as if losing interest.

'But this is all mere conjecture. How do you know it is drugs? I think the guards may have checked the food suppliers, at least on some occasions. They are expected to do that'.

Sekhar hurried to present the matter in a new light, to retain the then director's interest.

'But, madam, the problem is not only on campus. We think students are going to drug sessions outside campus too'.

'But that is outside my purview', Sujata responded firmly. 'Whether they go out to eat, or to the beach, or to do something else, I don't care. I am not their watchdog outside the campus. It becomes an issue only if their outside activities spill over to the campus, say, as drug-induced violence, etc.,'

Mohan and Sekhar looked at each other, uncertain how to respond. The meeting was not going as they had expected it to.

'One more thing, madam', Sekhar said, 'why are food packages delivered outside sometimes, not to the rooms where they will be noticed?'

'Outside? Outside the IIM gates?'

No, we have seen packets delivered outside the library building, in that deserted side of the building under the beehive, where no one goes'.

He was surprised to see the hint of a smile on Sujata's face. Why has she been told this piece of news already? Undeterred by this cool response, he continued.

'And there is also what the professor from Kharagpur, what is his name, said'.

'What did he say? What does that have to do with this discussion?' Sujata looked impatiently at her watch. Time to throw these nitwits out!

'That junkies and boozers are better people'.

Mohan tried to press home the advantage:

'In public, Dr. Das. To senior students. Bad influence on students, you agree?'

Now Sekhar gained more confidence and spoke up boldly, more loudly.

'Is that statement not a vindication of the use of drugs, madam? I would put it this way: it is an invitation to a drug-using fraternity?'

Sujata looked at him thoughtfully.

'Yes, I have to agree, Dr. Sekhar. But can we conclude that Dr. Saha is, therefore, a drug user himself, and is trying to win over students to his fraternity, as you put it? It may be an innocent ploy to capture attention, to become more popular, to stand out as a 'dashing' personality'.

Sekhar's face revealed what he thought of such an interpretation: a very far-fetched possibility. But he wouldn't dream of saying that to the director's face. But Mohan revealed his persuasive abilities once again:

'Dr. Sujata, you read reports about drug mafia here in Calicut?'

Then he added artfully:

'But Malayalam paper, you may not read'

'Mohan, you don't read Malayalam either', Sujata told him in an acid tone.

Mohan had not expected this direct counterthrust and was tongue-tied for a moment. But Sekhar came to his rescue.

'It's like this, madam. Some of us staff were all having tea together, and then the librarian read out the news from a Malayalam paper'. He cast an anxious look to see how Sujata was taking it.

'Go on...'

'It seems that drug addicts are occupying all empty, unused public and private spots public, and private spots in the city. People go away on vacation to come back and see drug addicts lying in a stupor on their balconies. And if you have an empty plot opposite to your house, the chances are that by evening a car or goods vehicle loaded with drugs is there'.

'So, the drug mafia has its tentacles all over the city, is it so? I thought Keralites had a problem only with alcohol'.

'That, of course, madam, is a perennial problem. But drugs are something new. Young men get addicted, and once in the mafia's grip, can never leave'.

'If you leave', Mohan broke in, 'then...'. He drew his finger across his throat.

'Empty private plots, you say', Sujata looked quizzically at Mohan, 'like the clearance below our giant beehive?'

Mohan was not prepared for that question and spluttered before answering.

'No, we do not mean that. Here outsiders in large groups do not enter. But delivery boys, yes'.

'Well, we could always keep watch on food delivery from outside. Which company or food delivery chain is it?'

'Salkara, madam', Sekhar answered. 'At least to begin with. It is a popular restaurant in the city and has opened an outlet in Kunnamangalam just downhill from us.'

'What do you mean, to begin with? Not anymore?'

Sekhar scratched his head and looked as if he regretted mentioning the company's name. But he had to go on now:

'It's like this, madam' his familiar refrain again, 'after observing Salakara food delivery at deserted spots on campus, the second-year student Ramakant reacted. He roughed him up a little, pushed him down from the bike, and all that'.

'This is monstrous, why was it not reported to me?'

'Dr. Sujata' Mohan hastened to correct any wrong impressions that his friend in arms had created. 'Ramakant is good boy, wants to stop drug problem. He is in our group for that'.

What group? Sujata found it hard to follow what Mohan was getting at. So, she continued to look at Sekhar.

'No one can take the laws into their own hands. I have to take some disciplinary action on this matter. And did the self-made sheriff Ramakant find drugs in the Salkara delivery box?'

Sekhar hung his face down. 'No madam, and after this incident, Salkara has not been delivering'.

'They deem IIMK unsafe, uncivilized!' Sujata gave a short laugh.

'No madam, it is not the company that has stopped delivery. The students still order Salkara food often. But now they call the new food delivery service, Swiggy, which can supply food from anywhere for a small charge'.

'They would be, of course having several individuals delivering, should be hard to pinpoint any particular individual for any funny business transacted on any particular day'.

Again, that strange look on Sujata's face that Mohan, whose ever-alert eyes missed nothing, found intriguing.

'Anyhow, I have noted your anxiety, and will take suitable steps'. Sujata got up briskly, indicating that the meeting was over.

After the duo had left, she did not immediately get down to the work to be submitted to the Ministry of Human Resources. It was puzzling, she thought, that Mohan had taken the extreme step of coming to her with a complaint about students and faculty members. He was quite capable of handling differences with either group on his own. So why bring her into the picture? She would be only a hinder in his path as he worked out situations and conflicts to his advantage, exacting concessions of various types from others. As to Sekhar, what she had seen of him during her sojourns with faculty members during student selection processes had not impressed her much. She still had in mind the ludicrous picture of him she happened to observe on such an occasion, after interviewing hours.

# IX

The student selection process at IIMK–and all the IIMs–comprised both a written test and an interview by a panel. The famous and dreaded written test, the CAT, used to be administered by each IIM separately. Faculty members would travel to each location with sealed trunks received from the central CAT committee and would return with the sealed trunks containing the answer sheets–of the multiple-choice types. It was a rather physically demanding duty, requiring the IIM groups to be at the location already by the early hours of the morning and to be watching and monitoring the entire process with the eyes of a hawk.

But much of the administrative burden of the CAT exam fell on the secretaries. It was they who guided the faculty members into allocated examination halls at the correct times and acted swiftly to prevent imminent conflict situations. Also, they, along with the faculty member in charge of the location, saw to it that each section of the CAT was given only the time interval allowed for answering it.

At times the strictly enforced time schedules of the CAT exam could be disturbed by unexpected occurrences. Once, as the exam was being conducted in a convent school that had kindly lent its premises for the purpose, a bell rang out at an unscheduled moment. A bell was always rung when the time allowed for each section of the CAT is over, but this particular bell was off the mark completely. All the secretaries and the faculty members administering the exam ran out of their exam halls in total confusion, and then only they realized what had happened: it was a prayer bell that had been rung from the adjoining chapel!

By the time Sujata came to IIM Kozhikode, the days of the physically administered CAT exam were over: the CAT went on-line. The other part of the selection process, the face-to-face interviews, continued, with hardly any differences in pattern from the earlier years. Again, the unobtrusive stage-management by the excellent secretaries was the steel frame on which the whole process was built upon. They ushered the faculty members to their allocated interview rooms, gave them the curriculum vitae of the candidates, evaluation sheets, even pens and writing pads. The approximate time at which the interviews would be over was also conveyed to the faculty members, projecting from how many candidates actually turned up; students who had already received calls from one of the older, more famous IIMs, wouldn't bother to turn up.

During the interview season, Sujata belonged to the jet age, the jet set, flying out to all the interview locations around the country. She made it a point to be present at every location for at least a day, to ensure uniformity in the interview process. For, otherwise, there was no saying that no location will throw up a bunch of selected candidates who were sub-standard. Left completely to the whims and fancies of faculty members, the most atrocious selection criteria, usually invented spontaneously on the spot, could be used with impunity.

Thus, it was so that on one occasion, when she was passing by an interviewing room, she heard loud singing. The premises where the interviews were taking place belonged to one of the international management institutes in Delhi, which was the regular site for the Delhi IIMK selection process. It was only a stone's throw from their hotel, and thus a very convenient location: they could even stroll back to the hotel for lunch.

Loud singing. Of the Carnatic concert variety, but with no accompanying instruments. Sujata opened the door and walked in. The faculty members, three of them, sat facing away from her. The singer, a girl in a formal pant and suit attire, saw her but did not stop singing. Perhaps she did not know that the recent addition to her audience was the IIMK director herself, though Sujata's face was often splashed out in the pages of the nation's dailies.

'No, that's not good, it goes like this'.

It was Kesavamoorthy, a faculty member recruited by the previous director who had interrupted the budding star.

'Sari-sari sa-sa-sa', "mooed" Kesavamoorthy. It was not sweet music for the ears.

'Stop it. You hear me stop it at once,' Sujata roared.

Kesavamoorthy turned around, shocked, and had to grasp the table in front as he almost fell off the chair.

'Is this an interview or not? What is going on? Sujata glared at the offending teacher, and then at the other two panel members. 'You are now fifteen minutes into interview time'.

Kesavamoorthy sat dumb, unable to respond to the

volley fired at him. It was Sugathan, the secretary allocated to that interview location, who answered. He had stepped into the room after hearing the commotion.

'Madam, yes, the interviews have begun. This is the first candidate, Miss Devika'.

'All right, I understand that. But why is she singing? Is this an unscheduled coffee break or something?'

Now Kesavamoorthy found his tongue.

'No, Dr. Das, it is like this: I asked Miss Devika here what her interests are, and she said that she is keen on Carnatic music. To test the truth or her statement, I asked her to sing, that's all madam.  No harm done; I hope?'

'No harm was done, my foot! The entire building was shaking as this concert went on, especially when you shouted that sa-sa-sa nonsense'.

The other faculty members burst out laughing but then put on a serious, concerned face when Sujata glared at them in turn. Kesavamoorthy regrouped his defenses and tried another tactic to redeem his interview methodology.

'You see, Dr. Sujata madam, candidates sometimes make exorbitant claims about their abilities and accomplishments. So, it is sometimes necessary to check their credentials on the floor, so to say, by whatever method is available at hand'.

'Bullshit'. Sujata didn't regret the foul word that came out of mouth involuntarily, though it was seldom that she used such words. 'And this test is your sa-sa-sa frog croak, is that so?'

Kesavamoorthy cringed visibly. He had not expected such a frontal attack from a lady director.

'Madam', he managed to protest feebly, 'I happen to be trained professionally in Carnatic music….'

Sujata did not let him complete his defense. 'Then resign and go to perform at the Chennai music festival. You will make more money than at IIMs'.

She left the room with that parting shot, but not before promising to look in again. After all, the interview day had only dawned, and there were at least twenty to twenty-five candidates waiting in line to enter each interviewing room.

The interviewing load on any particular day depended on the luck of the faculty members. Sometimes, on a lucky day, there would be only ten candidates or fewer to be judged, even though twenty candidates may have been listed. The ones who did not turn up would be usually the ones who deserved to be selected. They would not have turned up because they got an offer from IIMs A, C, or B, or XLRI Jamshedpur. IIMK was usually ranked after these four very established institutes, up from a rank of 11 or so at the time the Kozhikode institute had started so that an offer from those would cause absenteeism at the IIMK interview. With only ten candidates, the faculty members could usually call it day by lunchtime. They wouldn't be asked to shoulder the interview burden at any other interview room, as the day's activities would have been minutely planned for each group.

Indeed, the secretaries would plan each day's activities with great care and precision, taking the load off the faculty members in many respects. As the teachers strolled to the common hall after breakfast, they would be handed a file containing all the details of the candidates. Sometimes an approximate time for each candidate's interview would also be given, based on an average interviewing time of twenty minutes. Each candidate would also be announced and brought in by the secretary, as though a visitor was being ushered into the presence of royalty.

Each interview centre was allocated a faculty coordinator by the director, but this coordinator's job was simplified, even made superfluous as the secretaries stage-managed every minor detail of the interview process. And, when the faculty coordinator tried to take on some practical function, the result could be disastrous or comical. Thus, once when a non-IIM interview panel member asked for a writing pad, the faculty coordinator of that centre tore off a page of his pad and handed it over: 'here sir, take this!'. And, on another occasion, when asked about directions to the interview centre, which lay right next door to the hotel, the presiding faculty coordinator answered, 'just take a taxi!

However, at times, the faculty coordinator could steal the show, even eclipsing the all-in-all s ecretary. Sujata witnessed such a performance once when Rakesh was the coordinator at an interview centre. He had called for an assembly of candidates before the interview process, not a usual procedure, and made the common lobby of the host institute his playground in a sense. He moved between the hundred-odd assembled candidates talking and gesticulating, sometimes holding his head inclined sideways like a bird intently listening, sometimes turning on his heels abruptly at great speed like an acrobat. At one point during his discourse, he stepped on to the sides of the fountain at the centre of the lobby, balancing on one leg and stretching out his arm to the water stream as he spoke. Sujata smiled, watching, for she could see that the aspiring students were suitably impressed, probably to the extent of wondering whether they could be in the running at all, to share a campus with the flamboyant man now performing in front of them. However, the two IIMK secretaries present, though ever vigilant and also suitably impressed by the scintillating show put on by Rakesh, were whispering between themselves and laughing into the palms of their hands. The faculty members present, on the other hand, stood watching quietly, seemingly appreciative of the detailed information being given to the candidates by Rakesh along with the theatricals–that may be excused.

One problem ever-present at the interviews was, Sujata knew very well, that many of the students would have gone to training institutes to prepare for the interviews and group discussions. The result could be noticed even as the students came in to register for the scheduled interviews. Artificial gestures, exaggerated courtesy:

'You first, lady, please go ahead'This when the other candidate, even if a female, has just entered the room and is standing in line all of five meters behind the institute-trained candidate.

'And how are you today, splendid weather outside, isn't it?

This to the harried secretary, Sugathan, doing the registration, who has been so busy that he has not even looked out through the window that morning. Sugathan, normally of a cordial disposition, extended the registration form without responding to the pleasantry, not even looking at the candidate.

However, Sujata knew also very well from experience, that when things got heated up at the group discussion, the veneer of gentlemanly behavior could drop off all of a sudden, soft soothing tones transforming into growls and fangs becoming bare. On that same day after Rakesh's one-man show, she went by the interview rooms to see how the group discussions were progressing. She had a foreboding that things may not go smoothly despite the basic simplicity of that part of the selection process. The trouble was that, in group discussions, there would be several performers instead of the one-man theatre played out by Rakesh, and what's more, their theatricals would not be authentic as they would be only following a handed-out script by training institutes. Almost all the candidates would have gone through several months of training programs for entry to the IIMs, and group discussions and interactions were emphasized in that training. Sujata would almost choke when she noticed the blatantly artificial demeanour of some candidates.

But the true disposition of the candidate, refusing to be dammed in, would usually come out at some stage of the selection process. That same day, she entered one of the interview rooms unobtrusively and sat at the back of the room just when the group discussion had been flagged off. The first person to speak, almost jumping the gun, was a girl with closely clipped hair like that of a boy. She started at a very high pitch, literally screaming,

'I believe that we should first ask ourselves…….'

With such a calamity of a beginning, the stoppers had been drawn. The next one to speak, a plump, delicate-looking woman seemingly in her early thirties, struck a still higher pitch, interrupting the first speaker who protested to no avail:

'Let me finish, just one second, let me complete'.

Soon others joined the fray, forgetting all they had learnt at training institutes about the importance of coming across as a considerate individual willing to listen to differing opinions. It soon resembled the melee at a crowded platform just after the train has arrived.

That was when Sujata rose and stepped forward, screaming herself at the entire crowd in front:

'Stop it now, you hear me, stop shouting, all of you'.

Several shocked faces were turned to her at once. She gained control over herself and said quietly, but with the quietness of a graveyard:

'All of you may leave the room now. We will call you back shortly'.


Whenever Sujata remembered this incident, for some reason her mind went back to her days at Delhi with her mother–who was then the senior-most official in the ministry of commerce, second only to the minister himself, a political appointee. Those were the days of the imperial reign of Indira Gandhi. Her mother told her once laughing, under terms of secrecy, how things functioned in the parliament. As various items were read out, the MPs would be half-dozing, their heads lolling from side to side. Then a motion might be introduced. As the motion was presented for approval, the MPs would come to life, shouting and gesticulating. Enraged at the commotion, Indira Gandhi would slam the table in front of her, saying,

'Motion passed'.

At that, the MPs would subside back into their semi-dazed state.

Perhaps the behavior of the candidates at the IIM interview had set off a reaction from her similar to that of Indira Gandhi in parliament, she would think whenever she remembered that catastrophe of a group discussion; that story told by her mother may have had a stronger influence on her than she had ever imagined.

The group discussions–and hence the interview process itself–was always over by 5.30, if not earlier, unless something exceptional had occurred. The evenings were free for the faculty members, no planning needed for the next day. Family members were not allowed to accompany faculty members for the interview trips, but still, their presence was felt in the manner their husbands–or wives as the case may be – toured the city in the evenings fulfilling decreed family shopping demands. And, in a city like Mumbai, quite a few of the faculty members who sit with grave faces during the interviews go bar-hopping too, what with many sports bars with huge screens often just around street corners from their centrally located hotels.

Sujata got up from her swiveling chair and stepped on to the balcony, for a moment's respite from her cluttered desk. Not that she was embarrassed by the mess her table was usually in: she remembered always, when viewing her desk, the saying–supposed to have been said by someone who noticed Einstein's cluttered desk–'an empty desk indicates an empty mind'!

The view from the balcony was just stupendous, with the distant Wayanad hills visible–curiously enough–on an overcast day, not on a sunny afternoon. Though the new restaurant, meant basically for management training groups, offered an almost 360-degree view of the greenery surrounding the institute, she preferred the view from her balcony. The hill on which that balcony and the institute itself had been built was–she was told–once the happy hunting ground of foxes; that must be why, she smiled to herself, there was still a fairly large breed of cunning foxes in human form on campus! Leaning on to the balcony, her thoughts again turned to the student selection process, which had offered her unrivalled opportunities to study the behavior of her faculty colleagues.

The interview process itself kept changing over the years, with the organizations giving training to candidates for IIM entry trying desperately to keep up with the changes. One result of this was that the candidates often came up with identical answers to questions. On being asked 'who is your favourite author', the candidate blurted out the name of the author that had been recommended by the training institute. Thus, the answer was usually 'Ann Hayden' during the heydays of that lady author. Candidate responses to questions about what attracted them to the author were comical–because the answers were almost always identical, coming out in a trained rush.

Such observations prompted the IIMK examination panel to start including short essays by the candidate also to test his or her facility in the written language–something note tested by the CAT exam with its multiple-choice answer system. Here another comical part of the section process reared its head, the choice of topics for the candidates' essays. As any pre-determined topic would be quickly circulated by candidates that have gone through the process and included in the training kit of training schools, faculty members were asked to decide the topic on the spot. They, in turn, came up with an innovative' system of giving a few words, sometimes just one word, as the topic:  for instance, the topic was stated on two occasions as

"International Economic Integration",

and

"Hostile Take-overs"

These topics were gobbled up hungrily by the candidates, who had been told to expect such subjects for the essay. But the topic could be more troublesome, demanding a higher degree of imaginative thinking from the candidates. For instance, the topic given by Navaneetham, a faculty member in the economics and strategy areas, at the Mumbai interview centre was 'brother'. Just that:

"brother".

Perhaps Navaneetham was driven by his sentiments about his own family, and the candidates were the unfortunate ones to bear the brunt of the fallout.

Such a topic ought to have left the candidates bewildered, being neither here nor there, but here is where the innovativeness of the training institutes came to their rescue.  As soon as the system of essay writing became part of the IIMK selection process, these institutes made the candidates write several essays on several topics covering a broad spectrum of areas. The idea was that any topic given could be bent or twisted to be affiliated to at least one of the topics in which the training institutes had prepared the candidates. It was like the old story where a primary student could write in detail about cows, detail about cows, and when asked to write on green fields, he wrote that a cow was tied to a pole in the field–going on to write only about cows. And then wrote on cows.  In the case of the sublime topic 'brother' given by Navaneetham, one candidate used a training institute session describing Swami… Vivekananda's talk at the Parliament of Religions in Chicago that had begun with the wonderful words:

'sisters and brothers of the United States of America'.

Sujata sighed. There was no way, it seemed, of viewing a candidate stark naked, so to say, shorn of all the layers of coatings laid on by these competent and innovative training organizations. But if the candidates come in over-trained, the faculty members enter the interview rooms quite under-trained for the job at hand: this stood clear even from just one look at the individual grading sheets submitted by the selection panel members. Often there would be widely disparate grades, with outliers both upward and downward of a mean grade. It was obvious that faculty members were often grading based on one quality of the candidate that has impressed them or put them off the most. Looks, voice, dress, inability to remember numbers, a country accent, the length of the pause before answering questions, an upper class or lower class bearing, lack of knowledge or perfect information about the interviewing faculty member's alma mater, anyone of these could send the candidate's grade shooting in an upward or downward trajectory. Then it was a tough job to try to get the offending faculty member to revise his grade a bit towards the mean given by the rest of the panel.

It was proposed that the faculty member giving a really outlier mark should bring down his grade towards the mean, or raise his low marks towards the mean. This proposal was adopted but discarded at the very first attempt itself. On this occasion, it was Dr. Mishra who had given a grade one hundred percent lower than the average of other faculty grades. Presumably, he was , fuming because the candidate who suffered this at his hands had not written down the Euler expression that he had been asked for :

What! You don't know the Euler expression! Here you go, take 1 out of 10

Of course, the candidate probably deserved this for not being prepared for the question that had been widely circulated by those who had been interviewed by Dr. Mishra earlier.

At any rate, when asked to adjust his marks, Dr. Mishra flatly refused. The entreaties of the other members of the panel fell on deaf ears. This had happened before Sujata took charge. The previous director who had a different way of functioning built on avoiding conflicts and confrontations, decided not to press Dr. Mishra - to avoid any possible faculty revolt against his leadership. So, the whole idea of standardizing faculty grades given at student interviews was dropped.

And Mishra was not the only one, it pained her to understand, who had   outlier marks. She was passing by an interviewing room one afternoon as the interview panel members were just coming out of their tea break. Well, not all the panel members, for the conversation she overheard concerned a faculty member was still inside the room:

'Rakesh gives sky-high marks to good-looking boys'

'What a pervert', was her first reaction–and then she meant the speaker who was Sekhar.

She wondered later if there was any truth in the allegation, but then dismissed it from her mind as rubbish.

For, she knew the kind of personal remarks that are passed even at high-profile company director board meetings. One lesson she learnt at those meetings–she is and was a member of several company director boards–was that one should not take a break to go to the toilet: because when someone did, the other board members used his absence to pass disparaging remarks about him:

'So now he had gone to comb his hair, but he has got nothing left!'

And so on and so forth. Maybe just having fun at someone's expense, but then it is no fun for that person!

Then, when she heard Sekhar's remark, she stopped and said in a joking fashion:

'And for good-looking girls, Sekhar!'.

But Sekhar refused to give in: 'no madam, just for good-looking boys'.

Sujata was taken aback a little, but said as Sekhar went past with his teacup:

'Sekhar, remember, brains and looks go together often'.


Standing on the balcony, Sujata could feel the cool wind lashing her face. 'Like Diya', she thought, remembering that conversation, 'I could have told that to Sekhar now, for Rakesh would have surely scored Diya very high'. Besides, she thought, Sekhar was in no position to pass personal judgments on others, considering the embarrassing position he had- or might have - put IIMK in one evening after the interviews at Mumbai.

That particular evening, after the interviews, she had

expected everyone to be out exploring the city but was pleasantly surprised to see Rakesh in the hotel's lobby, leafing through some magazines.

'Oh, you are cloistered in the hotel - or are you receiving guests here?' she asked, looking around.

'Not at all, I have a dinner appointment with a friend, later at eight. Didn't want to stir out till then', Rakesh said, waving to her to sit down beside him.

'That's nice; all of us need a change from the routine. It has been a long day, isn't it, twenty-five candidates interviewed by each panel, right?'

'Not all that tiring really, Dr. Sujata', Rakesh said smiling. 'But, of course, a change in scenery is always refreshing. It's just that I have been around these parts so much that I don't feel like going out to explore like some of our other colleagues do. I thought I'd stay here, it is a pretty relaxing place in itself, till it is time for dinner with my old friend'.

It suddenly occurred to Sujata that she could probe him a little about how Divya was faring. She knew that Rakesh was spending a lot of his free time with that sensitive girl, left trustingly in IIMK's director's care by her parents.

'By the way, how is that girl Divya faring? I am asking because I know you two have something in common in being sports-enthusiasts. So, don't mistake me now!' Very uncharacteristically for her, Sujata leaned over and poked Rakesh in the ribs.

Rakesh seemed taken aback, more at the poke in the ribs than at the question. He sat up a little straighter before answering:

'Pretty good, I think she is doing well, Dr. Sujata. I find her to be very focused, doing everything according to her longer-term objectives, or final goal, whatever way you put it. The sports thing is part of that mental make-up, for developing the strength and energy for sustained efforts in other fields as well'.

'I see, stamina carried over from sports to academics, is that it?', Sujata laughed and Rakesh joined in. But he suddenly became thoughtful and leaned back, running a hand over his thick curly hair.

'It may be an odd thing to say, but I am a bit worried about her. For all her physical fitness and capabilities, she is a very sensitive person, easily hurt, I would imagine, even by mildly offensive behavior or talk'.

Sujata said nothing immediately, impressed by such an accurate reading of the girl by the faculty member. Then she said slowly,

'Interesting observation, Dr. Rakesh, what makes you say that?'

But Rakesh avoided an answer, opening and spreading out his palms as if to say he had no explanation to offer. As if to avoid further discussion on Divya's personality, he got up to his feet in a quick, smooth movement.

"I think I'd better make a move now. If I walk now to the dinner place, I will be just in time. A good swing in the fresh evening air will do a lot of good after sitting shut in a room the whole day!'

After Rakesh had gone, Sujata sat for a while in the lobby going through the magazines, he had left lying on the sofa table. Then she made a couple of calls, and straightaway went down to the hotel entrance without going back to her room to change or freshen up: a car would arrive shortly to pick her up, dispatched by a former colleague from IIM Lucknow, who was also in Mumbai on some work. Rather than waiting in the lobby, she preferred to walk up and down on the green lawns stretching on both sides of the hotel entrance.

It happened as she was about to stroll past the entrance for the third time. Sekhar - who was also in the interview panels allocated to Mumbai - ran in panting and stood behind the security guard's room, hidden from a direct view from the road, as if he was taking refuge there. There was a steady stream of passers-by on the road outside, as to be expected in the heartland area of a major city like Mumbai. Sujata could see nothing unusual happening outside the hotel. But then, suddenly, a bunch of men, six or seven, ran past the hotel gate shouting,

'Catch him, thrash the dirty scoundrel. Where is he hiding?'

Uncomprehending why the scene had suddenly become threatening, Sujata glanced towards   Sekhar, who was now crouching behind the security guard's cabin, well-hidden from the road. Only after the sound of the 'ruffian gang' had faded away into the distance did he step out and come over to her with a forced grin.

'What happened out there?' Sujata asked unable to make head or tail of the situation that had developed suddenly like a bolt from the blue. 'What was that all about? Were those people after you?'.

Realizing the incriminating nature of that question, she

added:

'I mean, were they trying to rob you or something?'

Sekhar clutched at that straw with relief. 'That's right Dr. Sujata madam. Pickpockets, that's what they are, the scoundrels; dirty scoundrels. One of them tried to snatch my purse, and when I resisted and pulled it back, the others attacked me. I had to run, literally for my life. They brandish knives too'.

'And nobody helped you? Usually, the crowd chases the pickpockets, and not the other way about', Sujata pointed out delicately.

Sekhar gulped, trying to figure out acceptable answers. 'You know how it is, madam, a gang, a mafia, who will face them?'

Seeing his tense face, Sujata felt a pang of sympathy, though she had a strong feeling that he was at least partly responsible for the turn of events.

'You are right, Sekhar', she said in a soothing tone, 'in a big city, no one was time for others, people turn a blind eye to what is happening right next to them'.

Sekhar disappeared immediately into the hotel to 'freshen up', as he put it, but Sujata knew that he was scared the 'mafia' as he put it, will come back that way past the hotel.


'Mafia'. That had word struck in Sujata's mind, resurfacing as she stood there on a wide balcony on the picturesque IIM campus. Pickpocket mafia or drug mafia? As she had told Sekhar, she knew for a fact that pickpockets do not chase people, even if they are in a gang.

The gang operates in passing on, say, a purse that has been pickpocketed, so that within seconds it is transported far away from the scene of the crime.

But a drug mafia could chase and mow down people, informers, or former gang members. Didn't Sekhar himself allude to the possibility of a drug ring within IIMK, that day when he came to her room with Mohan?

But the words 'dirty scoundrel', that the group of men was screaming: did Sekhar do something dirty out there that made him a legitimate target of a posse?

Did a raindrop blow on to her face, or had she imagined it? Her first rainy season in Calicut, at the IIMK campus, had been a magical experience. One evening then as she stood on the same balcony, she could see the rain sweeping in rapidly from the distant hills. No hint, no warning of a raindrop, it was a direct deluge. The rain had reached the balcony even before she retreated from the front railing: horizontal sheets of water sweeping in, not slanting, fully horizontal. She was drenched in an instant, but stood her ground, lifting her face to meet the waves squarely. When she came down the steps later to her car, the security guard and the driver were shocked to see her condition and tripped over each other trying to get her into the car and to the welcoming warmth of her bungalow.

Again her mind turned to Sekhar and his embarrassing predicament at the Mumbai interview centre. Could it have been the drug mafia that had been hot on his heels with murderous intent? After all, it was he, along with Mohan, who had raised the spectre of the drug mafia in their discussions with her, going out of their usually trodden paths at IIMK to do so. She pictured again in her mind the gang that had chased Sekhar. Pickpockets, whether chased or chasing someone, wouldn't resort to the use of such words as used by that gang. They may call someone 'chor', but not 'dirty scoundrel'. And, though, she had been reluctant to accept at face value Mohan's–and Sekhar's–claims to be altruistic, she had not brushed off their warning about the possible existence of a drug racket centred around IIMK. She did know from past personal experience that the drug problem could rear up like an undefeated devil at the most unexpected places.

Past personal experience.

Her father had died when she was nine years old and she had been brought up by her mother. A very capable and punctilious lady, she used to wake up Sujata at 5 Am every day to teach her mathematics and English, which she considered the core subjects. Perhaps Sujata got her 'never say die' attitude from her mother–whose favourite statement was:

'There is a solution to every problem'.

Sujata's mother held a very senior position at a ministry, and their living quarters consisted of a bungalow with sprawling lawns on Canning Lane, close to Connaught Circle. Their neighbours were folk holding similarly exalted government jobs, and the immediate next-door family had a son, Navin, just a year older to Sujata. It had often seemed to her that her mother had found plans of an eventual matrimonial alliance–involving her and Navin as the main performers - to strengthen the bond with the neighbours. She had nothing against it, never thought deeply about it, but it lay somewhere deep inside her as a fond thought– though not as a hope. Navin was a personable young man, sportsman as well as a bright student, with a ready, pleasantly chiming laugh.

She had finished her B.A commerce degree from Lady Shriram College and had been admitted to Manchester Business School for an MBA, a two-year course, rather than the one-year degree course prevalent than in Europe. After the first year, in which she had topped the class in most of the subjects, she came back home to Delhi for the Christmas vacation. She was surprised to see that her mother seemed to have cut off connection with the neighbours, never talking about or even alluding to Navin and his family. Slowly, the truth came out, after some delicate prodding on Sujata's part:

Navin had become a drug addict–as had most of the members of the Delhi University badminton team, of which he had been the top-ranked player. A tragedy of enormous proportions: the deadly virus had swallowed an entire group of young athletes at one go. Perhaps one player had become addicted first, and the others had been gradually lured into the death trap.

She saw Navin only once again. She was being driven to the International House to watch a dance performance when the car stopped at a signal. A long queue, they missed to green lights. That's when she saw Navin again. A thin figure in a torn coat was poking into the waste bin by the signal with a stick. She sensed, rather than observed, it was a person she knew. Suddenly, the man turned around and looked straight at her.

Then his gaze never left her face.

It was Navin: a pitiable version of him, all skin and bones and with a greyish colour to the face. She saw him framing silently a word with his lips:

'Sujata'.

There was neither sorrow nor joy in his eyes as he looked at her. It was as if he knew he was in a world separated forever from hers and he was having a last look.

She never saw him again, heard later that he had died in Delhi the next year as springtime decorated the city with flowers. Now when she remembered him, she thought that he was a good boy: a good boy for whom this world was too bad, not a boy who was too bad for this world. And, in moments like this, she knew that she was wrong in thinking that the sentimental part of her had withered away forever.

So, not a moment of laxity in watchfulness, she told herself as she wound up for the day and left the sprawling room with the spacious balcony. Vague, unknown threats seemed to lurk in the shadows–in that virtual paradise, the land of the green magic as tourist brochures put it. Unfortunately, she thought, it may be such places that attract parasites and criminals, for the bounty is richer in terms of the uncorrupted souls to be recruited for hell.

# X

'Clearly, Sujata madam's fears were unfounded',

Jose remarked to Bhaskaran as he sipped his glass of whisky. He had told the director,

'I promise to stay and watchful'.

But a couple of whiskies were not going to affect judgment. Of course, he would not place himself at the same level as Bhaskaran, who had been a Border Security Force soldier before joining IIMK and had a phenomenal capacity for consuming huge quantities of rum and being none the worse for that.

Bhaskaran, from whom Sujata had extracted no commitment to be sober and alert, probably realizing that she would be asking for the moon in doing so, did not grasp what Jose was alluding to–nor did he care. But he responded anyway:

'Yes, no one getting drunk, no fights, no hanky-panky'.

'I wouldn't say no hanky-panky', Jose answered, having seen a few such activities in the party hall.

The hall where the Fresher party was being held was the Vasco de Gama hall at the Taj hotel in Calicut town, which has sprawling landscaped lawns and gardens, and is a place one can get lost in with several tucked away parts to it. When Sujata's nephews of school-going age had visited from the U.S, they had stayed at the Taj, and had liked it so much that they were always making excuses not to go out of the hotel:

'What, go to Kappad beach with that driver? The way he drives? Did you see the way he overtook a truck on the way from the airport when another truck had almost come parallel from the opposite direction? No, thanks, we are spending the evening here at the Taj!'

When Sujata said she could organize another driver, the nephews again said in unison: 'no, thanks, no way we are going out with all these traffic blocks'. So, they stayed back at the hotel happily, moving from one spot to another.

The Vasco de Gama hall is usually divided into two parts by a screen at the centre, each part is large enough to accommodate medium-sized gatherings. But the screen had been removed for the Fresher party, which would have been considered a large get-together by any measure, even if not all the juniors and seniors turned up: clearly, the entire Vasco de Gama hall was needed for that function. In fact, for most IIMK functions such as conference dinners, the whole hall was always booked.

For formal IIMK dinners thrown by the director, no alcohol would be served. However, since the Fresher party is an informal one, like a private party thrown by senior students, the alcohol ban was not in operation that evening. Three or four tables with rows of various types of liquor were placed against the sidewalls of the hall. There were plenty of snacks too, especially of the seafood variety, but there were few takers for that: the students seem to thrive on the combination of potato chips and spirit, easily picked up during a pause in their animated chatting or dancing. Some girl students were also becoming bolder, perhaps alcohol-fuelled, and had started up inviting faculty members to bend a leg or two.

'Watch out now' Jose pulled his colleague's leg, 'someone might ask you up for a dance'.

Bhaskaran had not noted the growing boldness of the IIMk girl students in the party hall. So, he shook his sadly at Jose.

'Me? Jose, which world are you living in? Here in India women do not ask men to dance, the men invite them'.

'You think so? But then watch out, one of the boys may call you up'.

Bhaskaran laughed so uproariously that he spilled his rum on his shirt, but Jose persisted:

'You have such a colouful, orange shirt, Bhaskaran! Some boy may ask you to dance, mistaking you for a female'.

Bhaskaran laughed again, clapping Jose's shoulder so heartily that his whisky spilled over in turn.

I see that you are not taking me seriously', Jose said, mopping his shirt with a handkerchief. But listen to this joke that was forwarded to me on WhatsApp'.

'Be careful that you are not violating any copyrights rules', Bhaskaran warned his colleague and friend in all seriousness. There have been cases filed for circulating jokes and videos with copyrights protection'.

'Oh, I'm sure there is no problem with this one. All

my friends have received this on social media. It is about a British diplomat who gets drunk at all official dinners or parties. Once, true to habit, he got drunk at a diplomatic dinner at the city of Sau Paulo - oh I'm not sure which city was mentioned in the joke, maybe it was Rio or Lisbon. Let's say it was Lisbon'.

'What, you don't remember the city and the country in which the incident took place? How can you deliver the joke then?', Bhaskaran shuffled his feet, not wanting to be tied up for a long time with a lengthy joke, away from the drinks tables.

'Does it matter?', Jose was indignant. 'If the diplomat got drunk in Rio, he might have got drunk in Lisbon too, isn't it? So, the joke can apply to Lisbon as well'.

Seeing Bhaskaran shake his head sorrowfully, he continued:

'All right, now think of this. In his book, 'The Discovery of India', Nehru wrote that once he was travelling in the great plains of the north, he noticed a woman struggling along with a heavy load on her head, the sun beating down mercilessly. He then thought that he would strive to wipe away the tears off the unfortunate ones such as that woman. Now, does it matter what the woman's name was, or in which district of India the observation was made? Tell me Bhaskaran'.

A bit confused, yearning eyes darting to the rum bottle at the nearest table, Bhaskaran acquiesced.

'Go on Jose, tell the joke and get it off your chest'.

Jose brightened up. He reached out and held to Bhaskaran's shirt button as if to make sure he doesn't break away to join a nearby group.

'So, this British diplomat got drunk at a reception in Lisbon', he paused and looked at his colleague through narrowed eyes before continuing. 'Then he happened to notice a colourful figure in orange standing alone. He went up to the figure and requested a dance to the music together. But the person declined, giving pertinent reasons'.

Jose broke off, unable to control the laughter bubbling through.

"What reasons? Can you make it quick?'., Bhaskaran asked impatiently. This was taking far longer than he had even feared.

'The colourful figure said, "I cannot dance with you because: Firstly, you are too drunk. Second, this music that you hear is not a dance beat, it is our national anthem"'.

Jose broke off again, unable to control his laughter. Bhaskaran tried to ease away, but Jose tightened his grip on the shirt button and continued:

'And, finally, the colourful figure said, "the third reason is that I am the Bishop of Lisbon"'.

Jose laughed again and was pleased to see Bhaskaran joining in.

'So,, you think someone may be drunk enough to invite me to the dance floor. The only one who now looks drunk enough to that is our dear librarian, but he prefers the glass to the dance floor! Time for a refill for you?', Bhaskaran asked as he turned towards the drinks table.

All said and done, Jose was doing justice to his promise to Sujata: nothing that happened in the party hall was escaping his attention. He noticed the librarian moving around, leaving no one unattended by his alcohol-fuelled cordiality. But to his credit, he was a jovial man by nature, even when quite sober. His mother used to tell her friends proudly about her school-going son: 'he is so popular, when I see him coming out after school he always walks circularly because he has to speak with all the friends that surround him as he moves forward! Then he knows all about his schoolmates' families, where the dad is working, what the mother does, tells me if there has been a death or marriage in a friend's family, what each boy or girl brings for lunch, everything, there is nothing he is not informed about!' So, the man's exuberance was inherited right from his schooldays, and it was in evidence there at the Vasco de Gama hall too.

Seeing Divya standing alone, Roshan having deserted for the drinks table, the librarian walked over to her on rather unsteady legs.

'I see that you are not too rigid like most of the women here–I mean in Kerala, not IIMK. What is that you are drinking? Vodka or gin?'

'Sorry to disappoint you', Divya laughed. 'It is only Seven-up. MY parents will fall over if they heard that I started consuming alcohol after joining an IIM!'

Then, suddenly, a surprised look came into her eyes. She was looking intently at a girl who had joined a group standing close to her. The librarian, following her eyes, remarked,

'That is Shyama, a second-year student. Why, don't you know her? I thought you freshmen must have met all the seniors by now'.

'No, not all of them; I am sure though that I will, soon. Maybe even at this party itself'. Divya continued to look at her: the girl who had walked, rather, tottered, past her at night in the student residence with a dazed look, glassy eyes. The same girl now stood there with a half-emptied glass in hand, must have had a drink or two already. At ease, confidently, gracefully poised; what a transformation from the figure who had stumbled past her that night with unseeing eyes, oblivious to her presence, almost tripping over and hitting the lobby floor.

At the far end of the hall where it was separated by a wall from the main lobby of the hotel, was a stage. Not a make-shift one, a proper stage. Groups of students occupied it alternately to present impromptu performances, usually standing around one mobile phone, craning their necks to see the words to sing along. Not impressive or entertaining, Diya passed her judgment to the librarian. So, she clapped all the more vigorously when Rakesh jumped on stage and sang a solo, the old heartthrob song, 'Jamaica Farewell'. When she came to her senses Roshan was by her side looking at her with amusement, and a kind of secret understanding in his eyes.

She could guess what was passing through Roshan's mind, that she was infatuated with the flamboyant faculty member, and quickly changed the subject.

'By the way, Roshan, could you find out which faculty member has hired the house next to Shalini's?'

'No, how could I? he sounded apologetic. 'I know you were keen to know that. But can I go around asking 'who is the neighbor of the dance teacher living outside IIMK campus?' I am sure the personnel department folk will think I am corked if I enquire about the living quarters of all faculty members! I will have to name the faculty member to find his residence, so the process works the reverse way. Besides, who will know about a dance teacher living nearby?'

'Well, maybe she has arranged a marriage match for one of the IIMK staff', Divya said half in earnest.

'You have been seeing quite a lot of her, haven't you?', Roshan asked with a pleased expression on his face.

'That's right. I find it de-stressing to do that rather than hopping on to a jeep and roaming around in the city with a bunch of classmates. And, actually Shalini has promised to take me around the city as well'.

'That sounds great', Roshan seconded. 'It would take only a couple of hours: it is a small city, probably takes only ten or fifteen minutes to reach any part of the city from the centre'.

'Yes, Shalini did mention that too. Still, it is an old city, there will be plenty of interesting sights. I am told that the Samudiris, the dynasty that ruled the city, had one of the longest reigns of any royal dynasty in India. I have also heard that some streets look the same as when Vasco de Gama landed'.

'By the way, Shalini tells me that she has a new gardener', Roshan said with a straight face.

Divya laughed. Oh, she told you, is it? Yes, here is the new gardener right in front of you! But I don't go around clipping and cutting and reshaping the garden or anything like that. I just water the plants on the days I visit her'.

'I am glad that you don't take the role seriously'.

Roshan said seriously. 'Just look at the IIMK gardeners. They are overworked taking care of the luxurious greenery at every part of the campus. Anyhow, I am sure your help is much appreciated by Shalini. She has little time left over after her tuition classes and hiring a gardener means extra expenses for her'.

'By the way', Divya said with a naughty grin, 'when watering the plants, I also get to spy on her neighbor, on the goings-on at the house of the mysterious, as yet anonymous IIM faculty member. Some of her plants are right at the boundary wall, and I can see into the house through the windows'.

Then she corrected herself, 'that is, when the curtains are not drawn', a tense look coming into her face.

' But I have to tell you this too. A few times the tables were turned on me: I could sense that someone was looking at me, spying on me, from the windows on the upper floor'.

'My, my, what a regular spy tale', Roshan's laughter boomed out.

'Which books have you been reading recently, Divya?', he asked, but then became serious.

'Better be careful, Divya. You never know how people react, even to innocent curiosity or overtures. And, if criminal elements happen to come into the picture, they are capable of the most extreme cruelty, beyond our wildest imagination. So just keep away, don't think at all about that IIMK neighbor of Shalini'.

Divya protested saying it was he who was imagining things. She had wanted to talk to him about a few things, strange things, she had noticed about that morbid house, but decided to say nothing more on the subject, though she would have welcomed his thoughts on those matters.

Jose was having a hard time fulfilling the commitment he had made to the director. He had thought the party would end after supper. But food, though available in plenty and good variety, seemed to have been a minor ingredient in the party. The students took some food on a plate in passing, and usually never returned to the food counters, choosing instead often to present another song on the stage. The party went on in an unorganized fashion, and there was never a formal introduction to the new students. It was as if, it passed through Jose's mind, that the 'Freshers' party was just an excuse to have a party on a grand scale and the intention was not to welcome the first years formally to campus. He knew very well that small parties with small groups and alcohol involved - though formally banned on campus–took place every weekend at the IIMK campus.

And, this large-scale party also seemed to be breaking into small sub-groups. Bunches of students were drifting away from the hall to the grounds outside, and Jose found it impossible to keep track of all of them. Some students were moving towards the main lobby and beyond, where the bar and the restaurants are located. To Jose, it was fine if the students got drunk at the Taj bar, but he was concerned about them moving to pre-planned locations outside the hotel: he knew very well that hired jeeps may be standing at the Taj parking lot and outside for this purpose. If the students chose to do this, he had no way of knowing what more they could be up to, and a warning bell about drug dens went off in his head.

Just as Jose had expected, the Vasco de Gama hall was losing its party revelers at a fast pace and by ten PM it wore a fairly deserted look. 'What an impossible task is this that Sujata madam has thrown on my shoulders', he lamented, finding it impossible to 'keep his flock together'. But at the same time, he knew that he director had her own, sound reasons for doing so, since he had been sometimes present as a guest at the librarian meetings where the IIMK librarian had given free vent to all his–real or imagined - insights into the vices pervading his institute's campus. He could be present at those meetings because he was the one, as one of the senior administrators at the institute who had to organize their practical aspects, including flight bookings for the participants.

Oddly enough, Divya had the same intention as Jose, to keep track of the dispersing students, to see what they were up to. Her reason for that was however totally different from that of the secretary. She was keen to find out what Shyama would be doing after the party, for she had a premonition that she would be seeing that girl in a different incarnation again later that night at the student residence, something like in the story of Dr. Jekyll and Mr. Hyde. Therefore, she wanted to find out in which gathering she gets turned into that tottering figure with a hypnotized look.

So, as more students left the hall, with Shyama drifting along with one of the small groups, Divya followed discretely behind. Roshan was busy talking with a faculty member from the operations management area, and so she did not pull him along. Unfortunately, as her luck would have it, the corridor outside the hall was jam-packed with airline officers: The Taj is the favourite nest in Calicut of airline pilots and that evening one of their get-togethers was going on simultaneously on the lawns just outside the Vasco de Gama hall. Or, perhaps it was a party to which some pilots and hostesses had been invited, for only a few wore airways uniforms. Whatever it was, Divya was effectively blocked at the exit of the party hall (or: blocked at the party hall exit) for at least seven to eight minutes, and when she emerged unscathed from the crowd, she could see no sign of Shyama and her truant group.

From inside the hotel, she could hear the strains of a band playing; from the dining restaurant beyond the lobby, adjacent to the swimming pool, she guessed. One can always expect to see   some IIMK students around when a band is playing! So, she turned and entered the lobby, pushed open the swinging doors to the restaurant.

It was a Filipino band playing, with a girl in a miniskirt and a white, fluffy blouse, obviously a band member herself, functioning as a cheerleader, dancing in front of the band. The tables at the centre of the large room had been pushed away to make space for an impromptu dance floor. And, true to Divya's guess, many IIMK students were dancing there, with the cheerleader swaying between them and the band.

However, though Divya scanned the room thoroughly, she could see no sign of Shyama. The students waved over to her to come and join them on the dance floor, but she made no move towards them initially. But then she caught sight of a door at the farther end of the restaurant. The door was closed, but she knew that there was a so-called 'Board Room' beyond the door where even the IIMK director board meetings were usually held – the board members preferring to stay at the centrally located Taj rather than the IIMK campus with its rural setting. So, she walked fast towards that door through the dancing crowd, dexterously avoiding the hands of the students reaching out to pull her on to the dance floor.

Her logic was simple. The IIMK students were adept at finding hidden, tucked-away spots to conduct their private parties or have their secret rendezvouses. If the door to the board room is closed, and there is no board meeting of any kind going on there, then it was likely that, with a sizeable population of the students around, one of their truant groups had occupied the board room.

Divya knocked gently on the door and waited. No response. She knocked again and then gently pushed the door open.

Unfortunately for her, it was, indeed, functioning as a board room that night. Some very intensive negotiations must have been going on for no one to have heard her knocking at the door. But now, as she stood there gaping, she was met by the cold eyes of an elderly man sitting at the head of the table, facing the door. He was dressed formally in a dark suit and tie and his voice was even colder than his eyes.

'Who are you? What is the meaning of this intrusion?'

About a dozen people were sitting around the table, all of them men, except for a young woman sitting close to where Divya stood trembling. No one else looked up at her, were busy going through the papers in front of them.

'Sorry sir, extremely sorry, a mistake!', she gasped and closed the door quickly. She had meant to close it gently, but in her nervousness, it closed with such a bang that she wanted to run away from the spot. But on second thoughts, she did not leave the restaurant. What if Shyama was actually with the dancing group and has only gone to the ladies' room? So, she decided to stick around for a few minutes and, looking around, noticed an empty table to the left of the board room's door, by the large glass windows opening out into the swimming pool area.

She had hardly made herself comfortable at the table, swiveling around on the chair to see the pool more clearly, when she received some unusual company. The Filipino girl who had been the frontline dancer for the band suddenly appeared and sat down on the chair facing her. She was trying to answer a call on her mobile but then gave up with a laugh. Smiling at Divya, she said,

'People call from home about trivial things as if I was still around there'.

Divya smiled back. 'Are you from Manila?', she asked, that city being the only city in the Philippines she knew about.

The girl said some name Divya could not catch and stretched out her hand.

'Hi, I'm Rachel. Nice to meet you here in beautiful Calicut; or, what is it you say, Kosikode'. She mispronounced the name as all but people from Kerala do.

Divya laughed. 'You got that right. And I'm Divya'.

But Rachel could not leave the topic of disturbing phone calls and SMSes.

'Let me tell you something funny, Divya', she said, pronouncing Divya's name perfectly. 'The other day I got a call from the local household waste collection company back home. It got automatically forwarded to me here in Taj. So the guy talked about a pending payment, and finally asked: "so where are you, at home or gone to Manila?". I told him with no preliminaries, "no, in India". You know what, Divya, no sound, only deep breathing at the other end. It was a thunderbolt from the blue for him. Then I heard a sound, probably he fell!'.

Rachel laughed, revealing shapely teeth, and stretched out her hand to hold Divya's. A passionate girl who took everything life had to offer, Divya thought. And, a tingling, happy sensation pervaded her whole body.

'You like it here in Calicut', she asked, after taking a quick look around for Shyama.

'Oh, yes', the Filipino singer-dancer replied, 'best place I've been in, except the cruises'.

'Oh, the cruises, yes, I understand, in the Caribbean?'

'Among others. All cruises are great fun: it is as if one is on a floating luxury hotel, with several nightclubs and bars. You are not just performing; you are having a great party yourself. Also, you get to meet people of all possible nationalities'.

'You Filipinos are very international, that much I have grasped', Divya smiled.

'You said i. If you meet any Filipino group, you will find that their life partners come from several countries. We are open to all cultures. And, as you can see', she indicated her band members with a flick of her head,' we belong to different races too: Malay, Chinese, India, European'.

Divya didn't say it, but she had also heard about the international bent of mind of the Filipino people in another context, that for them, who tended to migrate a lot in search of lucrative work, paradise was at the other end of an intercontinental flight. Diya had a cousin working as a doctor in the U.S.A, and several of her colleagues were from the Philippines.

We have cruises from India too', she enlightened her newfound friend, 'off the coast from Goa, for instance. And, how long will you be singing here, will you be coming back again?'

'We are scheduled to come back again this year'. Rachel got up, raising a hand to her band members who were waving to her to come back. Divya looked her over. A perfect slim figure, with a mischievous look in her dark eyes that somehow seemed to complement her miniskirt that pivoted along with her body as she turned around swiftly. But somehow, she got the firm impression that, notwithstanding the bohemian lifestyle, the young Filipino was wise far beyond her age and a shrewd judge of character. 'That could be why', Divya thought with a touch of pride, 'she had stayed back to talk at some length with me despite the repeated calls from her band to resume duty'.

'I am sure we will meet then'. Rachel touched her hand before leaving. 'I can see that your student group is spending most of your time here at the Taj! But, wait, why talk about my next visit? I am around for some more time in Calicut, the night is still young as far as our current contract run is concerned. So, see you around!'

Still no sign of Shyama. Divya got up and, avoiding her dancing colleagues again, took the exit from the restaurant into the swimming pool area, which also hosted a fair-sized gym at the farther end of the area, away from the dining hall. The pool was empty except for a foreign woman, who looked European (why could be Filipino, Divya smiled to herself, remembering what Rachel had said), doing backstrokes in a relaxed fashion, very slowly, with closed eyes.

Is she meditating, Divya wondered as she walked the past the pool and entered the gym. No luck there either, no sign of Shyama.

She decided to check out the upper floor of the lobby-office area of the Taj. She had been once to the bar located on the first floor, a small but laid-back place overlooking the swimming pool and the palm trees lining the pool. So, she turned left after the restaurant doors and, walking along a long corridor lined with office rooms, took the steps leading to the bar. The bar lay to the left, past a table-tennis table where a few kids, a foursome, were having a great time, playing a game of 'rounders' where one has to cross over to the other side of the table after each shot. As to be expected, there was a group of IIMK students sitting at a table discreetly placed, away from the glass windows opening out to the pool, not visible from the entry. Diya could only catch sight of them when she went past the screens separating that part from the rest of the bar. The students were talking seriously, in low voices. She wondered what mischief they were up to, but didn't stay to find out. She had to find Shyama, somehow that felt urgent.

She had meant to go down at once to the parking lot to look into the jeeps hired by the IIMK students. For some of the students had opted to organize their transport, to be not dependent on the institute bus and its timings. But as she came out of the bar, she remembered that there was a conference hall on that floor also, smaller than the Vasco de Gama hall. It lay beyond the table tennis table, a little after the washrooms to the left. So, she walked up the hall, stopping for a while to look down at the lawns directly in front of the entry to the lobby, which seemed to get rapidly populated by spill-overs from the airline's party further away.

There was no sound at all from inside the conference hall. Clearly, no programme had been scheduled for that day. She was about to push open the entry door when it opened and Rakesh came out. With him was his constant companion from the first year, Diya could never remember his name.

Rakesh looked a bit startled on running into her at that off-the-beaten-track place, but said immediately:

'Where are you going, Divya, there is no one there? We had mistaken this room for the bar'.

'Really?', it was Divya's turn to look surprised. 'But how could you miss the signs? It says in big letters to the right of the table tennis table over there: Bar, open 11 a – 11 pm, happy hours 11 am to 6 p. You are too late to be made happy, right?'

Rakesh and his male companion both burst out laughing, the boy squeezing his teacher's arm. 'You made a point, Divya, we are too late to get the happy hours discounts, and the prices are steep without that. So, I think we will check out the gym. It is too crowded at the drinks counter at the party'.

'Not any more', Divya pointed out. 'But it won't be fun

going back there, most people have left. But the bus is still there for the trip back'.

Who is corrupting whom? She wondered as Rakesh and the boy turned away and entered the bar after taking a good look at the 'happy hour' timings–for future reference, no doubt. Is that student a heavy drinker? Maybe he has been influenced not by his professor, by Kerala's culture of excessive alcohol consumption, about which she had been warned before leaving for Calicut.

She went down to the main lobby again and then through the exit door. Her destination this time was the car park, located at the extreme left edge of the front lawns. Perhaps she could 'catch', at least get a glimpse, of Shyama and her group before they left the Taj grounds. With luck, she may also be able to get some clue about their plans for the rest of the night.

But she was too late. When she was still some fifty meters from the car park, the jeeps hired by the students swung out at high speed into the entry road and out through the gate. The jeeps were filled with IIMK students, and, in one of them, feet dangling out into the air, sat Shyama laughing and screaming out something at students sitting in the interior.

I am sure I'll be seeing her much later tonight, in her other incarnation, Divya thought, looking at the disappearing backs of the jeeps. She was about to turn back to the hotel when she heard the sound of a motorbike. The bike too took a sharp turn out of the parking lot and sped away, in the same direction as the jeeps.

She could get a good look at him, in the illumination provided by the lamps around the parking lot; even though much of the face was covered by the helmet, she was sure that it was the Swiggy food delivery man again. And, for the first time, she paid attention to the bike he used: a Royal En Field Bullet, rather unusual in the delivery scheme of things, where skimpy bikes, even mopeds, were commonly seen.

Divya walked back to the Vasco de Gama hall. The crowd in the corridor in front of the hall had evaporated. The hall itself was nearly empty, but for a few staff members and the conscientious secretary, Jose. He came up to her and asked if she was ready for the bus ride back to IIMK.

'Not much point in staying on', he suggested. 'The only people left here in the hall are those who live around here, in the town itself. They won't need any transport; so, what do you say, Divya, shall we leave on the institute bus? It's up to you'.

'So, are you staying on campus, Mr. Jose?'

'No, but close by. I have a rented house, rent paid by IIMK', he laughed. 'And, I have plans to buy that house provided by the owner is willing to part with it for a reasonable price. I am from further south in Kerala, but, as the saying goes, once you come to Calicut, you never leave!'

'Sounds good', Divya said doubtfully, the MBA student in her coming to the fore, 'But keep in mind that the presence of IIM will drive up the real estate price rapidly'.

'No doubt it will', Jose shrugged his shoulders. 'One has to accept the inevitable. But your point is a good one. We have a ready example to underline what you said: a single institution in Thrissur changing the entire landscape of the city'.

'I guess you are referring to the economic landscape'.

'Sorry, you are right, I mean the economic landscape. You see, a suburb of Thrisoor was a sleepy place until one P.C. Thomas started a coaching centre for civil service examinations, later diversifying into entrance examinations for medicine and engineering. So, IIT, IAS, the works! It became very popular, with students renting places to stay, their mothers often accompanying them. So, the place got an economic…,' he stopped, 'what you call that?'

'An economic fillip?'

'Yes, a virtual economic boom. Prices went up, but there was also genuine economic expansion, with all kinds of activities starting up to serve the expanded population'.

'I am sure that is going to happen in the IIMK area too, in sleepy Kunnamangalam', Divya smiled.

'It's already happening, Divya, it's already happening. I have seen remarkable changes in the few years since I joined IIMK. So, back to business: shall we go to the bus?'

Bhaskaran, who lived in town, had already left on his trusted vehicle, his bicycle. So Divya and Jose walked over to the bus which was parked on the road near the Taj's exit gate. Some students were already sitting inside, poring over their mobile phones. Not many, but perhaps one-fifth of the total student crowd that attended the party. The rest had gone on to further nocturnal adventures, in the jeeps that Divya had seen and many more.

'Let's go', Jose told the driver, as if he had read Divya's thoughts. 'We are not expecting any more'.


Divya stayed up late watching a movie on her computer.

She wanted to stay awake; the night was still young on campus. If possible, she wanted to catch sight of Shyama once more that night, to see in what condition she was in.

It must have been around one o'clock that she stepped out of her room to go to the water fountain at the lobby on her floor. She had waited till the music blaring out from one of the rooms had stopped abruptly before leaving her room. She sipped some water and then stood gazing out at the thick foliage behind the building.

Suddenly she heard an unsteady patter of feet sounding closer and closer. It was Shyama, half-running, but staggering along. She had come from the corridor at the far end of the lobby and was headed towards the staircase leading down. But, reaching the staircase, trying blindly to catch the railing, she started to fall. Literally sprinting in, Divya managed to catch her as she fell – and saved the girl from a serious head injury.

There was no response in the glazed, staring eyes of the girl; so different from the eyes full of life and mischievousness that had captured Divya's attention at the Vasco de Gama hall. She didn't seem to recognize Divya. However, she did mutter something that sounded like 'thanks', before extricating herself from Divya's hands and proceeding down, holding precariously on to the railing.

Divya stood there at the top of the staircase, staring after Shyama, wondering whether she should go along to help her. But the girl had pushed her away forcefully as if indicating she didn't care for further help – or, she may mean, interference. It was a delicate situation and Divya opted to stay where she was, listening intensively for any sound of a body hitting the floor. After a while, she went back to her room, wondering whether she had heard right:

*Did the distraught girl have enough normal consciousness remaining in her to have muttered 'thank you?'*

# XI

A few weeks after the fresher's party at the Vasco de Gama Hall, Divya was on her way for her usual weekend visit to Shalini, skipped over for consecutive weeks due to IIMK academic pressures. This time she did not take her usual short-cut via the beehive area: she had reasons to do so, having had a nasty experience on her previous passage through there.

On that day, dusk had already fallen when she walked past the desolate, unkempt green lawns underneath the giant beehive. She was surprised to see a car parked there with emergency lights blinking, close to the massive wall of the computer building, not visible from the adjacent avenue.

'Is there anyone in the car', she wondered. 'And why are the emergency lights flashing, is it a call for help?' To add to her confusion, the car was shaking rather vigorously from side to side.

She went close to the car and peered in, but nothing was visible through the thick tinted window glasses.

'Perhaps the windows are drawn down on the side close to the building', she thought, and went around the car, brushing the building wall as she did so.

Sure enough, the backseat window on that side was pulled down a little on that side. Projecting out through the window, flailing in the air, were two shapely feet, only one clad in a shoe with a bit of a high heel to it.

Divya went closer and tried to peer inside, asking,

'Hello, do you need any assistance?'

Then she recoiled back as if thrown back by an electric shock. A female voice raised in high pitch screamed at her:

'Get lost, you interfering bitch!'

She didn't stay therebeside the car anymore. Realizing that she was intruding upon an intimate, private act, even if in a public place, she ran, skirting the car, and did not stop until she had reached the back gate of the institute.

Stopping at the gate to catch her breath, she wondered,

'Was it Shyama there in the car?'

The flailing feet had reminded her of Shyama's colourful exit from the Taj grounds on the party night. But the voice? The voice had sounded unfamiliar. She had heard Shyama speaking at the party in a fine, modulated voice. It seems unlikely that such a girl could have screamed obscenities in a screeching voice. Unlikely, she told herself: no, it was not Shyama.

This time, taking another, longer route to the back gate, she came upon a clearing in the thick foliage lining the avenue where a boisterous party seemed to be in progress. A student, his bare upper body a mixture of muscle and plump fat, was dancing to a Bollywood beat and egged on by a group of clapping and shouting students, a girl in skimpy shorts and just a bra above, was stepping in rhythm to him. Divya didn't know those students by name, but she thought the male student was a senior named Ashok. A typical Bollywood dance with a lot of sidestepping and arm movements. Seeing Divya, some students shouted to her to join the fun. She saw Shyama in the group too, could distinguish her voice rather melodiously raised, urging her: 'come on over'. Divya smiled and waved back, targeting Shyama, but quickened her pace and left the spot.

'So, it wasn't Shyama that evening doing acrobatics in the car', Divya told herself, with an unaccountable feeling of relief about that conclusion. 'She seemed to harbor no ill feelings towards me, so it couldn't have been her!'

'But it could well have been that other girl - doing the Bollywood dance in her bra - in that car shaking from side to side', she figured unreasonably, but then pinched herself as if to say, 'don't be illogical now'.

She looked down at her hand to make sure she hadn't dropped the package she was holding in waving back at the celebrating group. Yes, it was there all right, though for the life of her she could not understand why she was carrying at all: a package from one lady to another, total strangers to each other, with she, Divya acting as the courier; A product of her trip to the small town of Pattambi for her social development project in microfinance.

IIMK, as distinguished from the other IIMs in the country, has a compulsory social development project that has to be completed over the entire two years of the MBA program. Anywhere from two to four students can take up one project. In Divya's case, she had opted for a project in microfinance, teaming up with Roshan.

The project is located in the hamlet of Pattambi, a small town situated on the banks of the Bharatapuzha river, called 'Nila' in popular parlance as well as in poetry. The town, about an hour and a half from Calicut by train, is considered a haven for retired civil servants, though not to the same extent as Ottapalam, a town lying a bit further away on the shores of the 'Nila'. They had traveled to Pattambi the previous week, after fixing an appointment with the owner-CEO of the microfinance firm chosen for their project. They were not expected to finance the project but were to provide management expertise and long-run planning. Finding sources of additional finance and avenues to market the products of the enterprises covered by the micro-financing scheme would be also very welcome input from the IIMK students.

The owner-CEO of the microfinance firm was a retired civil servant, and the microfinance firm was based in one wing of his large ancestral house itself. Both he and his lively, outgoing wife were at the station to receive the IIMK students. The man was solemn-looking with an earnest face and a trimmed military moustache. He introduced himself by a name neither Divya nor Roshan could catch, but his wife stepped up and gave Divya a small embrace, saying, 'and I am Devi'. She must have been in her late forties, but looked not a day older than thirty-five, with jet black hair and a voluptuous body, dressed in traditional Kerala style, draped in a kasavu mundu, not a chiffon sari.

'So happy you could come', she said taking Divya by the hand. 'Shall we go straight home, Sukumar ettan?', she turned to her husband, in the process making his name clear to the students.

'Of course', he answered, adopting a business-like tone. "The women are already there waiting'. Not clear if he meant a reception committee of women, the students, their t-shirts proclaiming their IIMK affiliation to the world at large, got on to the Innova car that arrived as soon as their host waved a hand.

When they reached the couple's home, the students were glad to note that the entrepreneurs waiting to meet them were all women, not a single male amongst them. The students joined them in drinking the proffered tender coconut water, drunk straight off the coconut with a straw, and the meeting started at once, wasting no time in preliminary formalities. There were not even any individual introductions made.

'We only work with women', Sukumaran said in a low tone to Roshan, 'much more dependable than men in terms of repayment; especially with the backing and promptings from the co-operative society that they have formed'.

The women were engaged in a rather bewildering spectrum of activities, ranging from candlestick manufacturing to textiles. One firm was even engaged in producing nuts and screws. To keep the proceedings short, they were asked to present the most serious problems they faced in running their businesses. The students noted that the problems were more or less universal to that group repeated by each of them. The main persisting issues were;

- Lack of marketing technique and support
- Too little capital, loans given by the microfinance

firm not adequate

- Draining away of capital for unavoidable consumption needs

- Husband's interference

Yet, despite the problems faced, the women were bright-eyed and optimistic, seemed to feel that they were taking part in a novel experiment. Many of them were Tamil-speaking immigrants of a lower economic class and had raised their families' financial status gradually by hard work in temporary employment. They were full of admiration for Divya, a girl who had found a place in such a haloed institute as IIMK. They did not disperse before she gave them an informal pledge to meet them soon again– with her advice on running their firms.

'What do you say, Divya', Roshan asked when the women entrepreneurs had gone. 'Are you thinking what I am thinking? That the micro-financing capital given to them is too low? 5000 rupees: a mere pittance'.

'Yes, definitely inadequate', Divya responded. 'It will have to be raised to 10.000 at least, preferably 25,000'.

But the financier was doubtful. He pointed out that with less capital per firm, he could finance more activities, more entrepreneurs. Besides, he suggested, the tendency to spend the capital for consumption is less when only small amounts are involved.

No, no, a separate consumption loan will be required for important personal consumption spending such as the marriage of their daughters', Roshan told the financier. 'Then there will be no danger of the capital amount–and the initial profits - getting spent on consumption'.

The IIMK duo was happy to see that the CEO was open to all suggestions, and could be persuaded to raise the loan capital without pulling the rein on his plan to bring in more women into the financing net. So, to them, the prospects looked bright for a fruitful relationship with the financier and a rewarding project for all concerned, including the student adviser–Rakesh, in their case.

They were taken around the ancestral property of the family after tea. A large piece of land, right on the shore of the Nila river, which must be that which gave the company its name, 'Nila Microfinance'. In the centre of the property lay a huge pond, the likes of which are rarely seen these days. Both Roshan and Divya fell in love with the pond and also the concept of having a large water body attached to living quarters. Roshan undressed and draping a towel too small for him around his midriff, jumped into the pond and proceeded to first show off his prowess as a swimmer, and then float  in peace on the water surface. The host family watched him with love and affection in their eyes and the lady elicited as much information about Roshan as she could out of Divya.

After Roshan had climbed out of the pond and was being a spot of 'liquid' refreshment by the CEO of the company, the lady of the family took Divya aside.

'Is your friend alone in Calicut or does he have a family of sorts there? You know a host family or something like that which Indian students are offered when they study abroad?'  Then she hesitated a little and asked a direct question:

'And, if you will pardon me asking, you two are not engaged or anything like that, are you?'

Divya laughed and couldn't stop laughing for a long minute. Then she enlightened lady:

'No, there is nothing between us, only professional relations. To answer your earlier question, he does have a 'chechi' in Calicut near our institute. So he is with her often'. Divya didn't bother to explain that she was using the word 'chechi' as is common in Kerala when referring to a lady friend, and not in its literal meaning as a sibling, elder sister.

'Oh, that's nice', the woman said, bubbling with enthusiasm. 'Perhaps we will meet her too. Why don't you bring her along when you come next, which will be very soon, I hope?'

Then she went off at a tangent. 'Too bad my daughter is not here. She would have enjoyed meeting you. She is away, doing a degree in fashion technology in Pune '.

Going to the showcase in the living room, she picked up an album with pictures of her daughter, seemingly a vivacious person like her mother. Roshan, who had come back refreshed and re-dressed, also looked at the pictures– which seemed to have made Devi, the host lady, very happy for some reason.

Divya was not put off by the woman's curiosity and naïve approach. She rather liked it. Evidently, though moving in exalted civil service circles in Delhi, the woman had not lost her native simplicity and love of life's simple pleasures.

But she was taken aback when, just when she had stepped out on to the porch to leave, the woman came up to her and extended small packet.

'Divya mol (little daughter), do me a small favour.

Please give this to Roshan's chechi'.

'Of course', Divya said, but wondering why the lady was sending a gift for a total stranger.

'Tell her I gave it; it is a personal item'.

Divya took it a bit reluctantly. What could it be, a lucky charm? But she could hardly say no to such a small request. But then why no lucky charm for herself, the courier?

Her intuition told her that the woman would like her to keep the errand a secret. So, she cached the package away in her handbag along with her items without Roshan or the lady's husband noticing it.

'I was telling Roshan that very few houses have ponds these days', the host and the CEO of the firm, Sukumaran, told Divya, shaking his sorrowfully. 'A pity, because it is good for the environment also; raises the groundwater all around, is a haven for birds and many other living things'.

'You know how it is', the woman chimed in, impressing Divya with her simple, direct, clear mind. 'The family properties had to be partitioned when the joint family system collapsed. The ponds stood in the way, had to be filled in for the divisions. Also, the price of property shot up so that keeping the ponds meant a loss of high income from the sale of land'.

'So, we are privileged to have visited such a rare ancestral property', Roshan said gravely. He stepped down from the porch. 'And, we look forward to working with you. It will be a very rewarding project for us'.

'Yes', Divya quipped, 'perhaps the best project at IIMK!'

Everyone laughed, the woman's laughter ringing out in a rich peal as she gazed with affectionate eyes at Roshan.

So now she was on the way to deliver the packet to Shalini, having taken it out of her handbag where it might lie forever unless the errand was handled immediately.

126

# XII

Walking at a fast pace, she turned the curve that leads to the straight stretch of some fifty meters to Shalini's house. Even from that distance, she could see two figures standing at the front gate of the mysterious neighbour's house. Narrowing her eyes, she could make out that one of them was none other than the one who had become her constant companion, the food delivery firm's man. His Royal Enfield Bullet had been left leaning against the plants along the sidewall of the house. The other was a woman she had not seen before; in fact, she had not seen anyone at that house or its grounds earlier. Placed next to her against the sidewall was a broom with a long handle, of the type used to clear away fallen leaves. Probably, a part-time housekeeper, Divya guessed, the one that Shalini had mentioned.

Suddenly, she heard the screech of tires. She had been keeping to the right side of the road to face oncoming traffic, obedient to the pedestrian instructions splashed on the backside of every city bus. But, looking back, she saw a large car hurtling along the uneven road surface, keeping to the extreme right. Sensing acute danger, she started sprinting towards a heap of granite stones kept against the sidewall which–she imagined - could be used as a launching pad for a leap over the high wall. She had just jumped on to that heap and turned around to keep track of the car, when it swerved away without smashing into the granite stones–and her. Through the lightly tined window pane, she saw a pair of baleful eyes glaring at her.

She slowly stepped down from the granite heap. Maybe the danger had been only in her imagination. When almost upon her, the car had turned away. He could have rammed into the granite heap, injuring her grievously also in the process, if not killing her. But wasn't it so that her lightning-quick response had saved her?

She looked towards the couple closeted in conversation by the gate of Shalini's neighbour. The man had been looking at her, but had then turned his eyes away and resumed the dialogue with the woman. They didn't look at her at all when she opened Shalin's gate and walked towards the front porch.

'What on earth is he doing here?',

Divya wondered. All kinds of wild thoughts raced through her mind. Is he trying to open up a sourcing point for drugs in that residential locality, or has he already done that and is checking outcomes? Or is he chatting up that woman, just a street Romeo? Or is he pumping her for information about Shalini and her routines, if so to what purpose?

'But two can play that game', she told herself. 'I could strike up an acquaintance with that woman and pump her for information about that house and its mysterious tenant!'

Then she suddenly remembered that what Shalini had

said–that the neighbour had a part-time male housekeeper. It must be then so that the male employee had left for a full-time position somewhere and this woman had been hired for the vacancy, probably on a full-time housekeeper-cum cook.

The sight of the food delivery man, again materializing as if out of nowhere, true to his style, had driven the fearful experience she had just had out of her mind. Now as she walked down the path lined by plants with yellow and red flowers in bloom, she realized that her heart was still thumping. It was a narrow escape: the car missed her by inches. But it was puzzling why it did not ram into the heap with her conveniently positioned on top of it. Could it be that the driver who–she believed–clearly had deadly intentions, only wanted to frighten her to begin with, with a warning message:

"Keep away"?

Before entering the house, she stole a look at the pair engrossed in conversation near the gate. Again, caught in the act, the man averted his eyes and turned to face his companion, who was talking animatedly, squarely.

# XIII

As it happened, that 'lucky charm' packet given by the charming lady from the microfinance household in Pattambi never got opened during that visit of Divya to the Shalini household. They were so busy discussing her 'narrow escape' that the packet lay forgotten on a windowsill in the living room. Shalini believed that the young boys who got their first licenses were so very rash and aggressive on the road–and that one such person must have been behind the wheel of the car that went berserk on the road outside that day. In other words, it was just aggressive, careless driving, not a deliberate attempt to harm anyone personally. Divya didn't try to correct her, though she was convinced that the driver was, indeed, trying to run her over. True, the car did swerve away at the last second, but that could be because the driver didn't want to smash the car against a pile of granite. The other possibility, again, was that it was a warning to her, to mind her own business at IIMK and its surroundings.

By now her friend must have gone through the contents of that packet, Divya thought as she reached Shalini's house again the following Sunday evening. The nerve-racking experience of the previous visit hadn't deterred her. She was the type that preferred to meet any danger face to face, was a fearless person by nature. Only some very discerning people like Sujata had perceived the very sensitive - and therefore vulnerable - inner core of that young girl who was on the recovery path from a  crisis earlier in life. But, as she walked now on the straight path leading to Shalini's house, she kept turning around, as if to be able to do precisely that: meet danger face to face, not letting it creep up on her from behind.

When she opened the gate of the house, she was quite surprised to see two little girls, numbering among Shalini's several dance students, there, running around playing 'catch me if you can'.

'What are you girls doing here?'

She stood between them to stop the game, and asked again, 'Why haven't you gone home after classes? And where is Shalini chechi (auntie)?'

The girls laughed, running around her to continue the game, but one of them answered, pointing a finger at her playmate:

'Rashmi's mummy is picking us up. Shalini chechi left to see a friend admitted to Nirmala hospital'.

Nirmala hospital was a reputed, service-oriented hospital that also ran a part

time clinic at IIMK. Divya knew that IIMK students were often admitted to the main hospital too, since the part-time clinic had doctors only on brief visits.

She was disappointed but told the girls that she would

keep them company till Rashmi's mother arrived.

'Divya chechi, then you can also come with us to get chocolates'.

'Chocolates?', Divya laughed. 'We must walk to the main road for that. Were you going to go that far by yourselves? Naughty girls, I will tell your mummies'.

'No, not to the shop, we are not that stupid', the girls screamed with laughter. 'To that house', they pointed to the next house. 'The uncle there gave us chocolates last week when we were waiting at the gate. Now Pushpa has just gone with him to get chocolates for all of us. But we can go there now if you come'.

'What!', an involuntary scream escaped Divya. Then, in the very next instant, she took off at a sprint and rushed in through the gate of the neighbouring house, which was half-open. By the time she reached the porch, her breath was coming in short gasps. She banged on the front door, shouting, "Pushpa", "Pushpa", come out, let her out'.

There was no response. The house lay deathly silent. She backed off a little to the edge of the porch to see if she could see in through a window.

Just at that moment, the door opened and Pushpa came out smiling. She had a bag of chocolates in her hand.

'See Divya auntie, what the uncle gave me'.

Divya embraced the child, tears filling her eyes. Then, holding the little girl behind her, she moved to the front door again. But, when she was about to bang on the door again, to confront the 'uncle', she thought better of it. She couldn't get into trouble herself when the other girls were left unprotected.

So, she held Pushpa tightly by the hand and walked swiftly away, without looking back. When she entered Shalini's gate, the girls came running towards her, laughing happily.

'Listen, listen very carefully, children', she started saying in a stern voice. But she was so agitated that she was spluttering, the words did not come out clearly. 'You cannot go inside that house for all the chocolates in the world!'.

But the children couldn't see why.

'No, chechi, he is a nice uncle. He patted our heads and said we are good children'. They added defiantly, 'We can go there'.

Divya kneeled, holding their heads together and crying softly. Then she managed to calm down and said in a very grave tone,

'Yes, you are very sweet children. There's no doubt about that. But please listen, sweet children, never talk to strange people, never take sweets from them. The sweets may put you to sleep and they will then take you away.'

She felt she had to frighten them badly: there was no other way to stop them from going to the next house, or from going along with strangers.

'Never go to that house or any other house unless Shalini chechi or I or your mother is with you. If you go to that house alone, a great ugly bhootham, ghost, will devour you'. She made a terrifying face and pretended to swallow something.

'Ayyo amma, mummy', the girls burst out crying. 'I want to see mummy now itself. Bad chechi!'

Divya patted their heads.

'There, there, nothing of that sort will happen to you if you are careful. Tell me that you will not go to that house alone'.

'No chechi, we won't, we promise', the girls cried out between their tears.

"Good girls, that way you will be safe and happy and you can have plenty of fun'.

Then she remembered something: she was going to talk to Shalini about possible performance by her children's dance troupe at the concluding day of an international conference to be held at IIMK and the Taj. A mention of this might cheer up the now despondent girls.

'By the way, would you like to dance on a real stage, with the audience clapping and cheering for you?'

'Oh yes!', the children cried in unison, 'yes chechi!'

"Good. I will arrange it with Shalini chechi'.

It had been Rakesh's idea to ask Shalini whether she could let some of her dance students perform on the last day of the conference with Indian as well as many foreign delegates. The conference was to be jointly organized by IIM K and an economic society, 'The Mediterranean Economic Forum', that was an amalgam of several societies from the various southern European nations. The host, of course, would be IIMK. The conference delegates, Rakesh said, would love to see amateur dancers, especially school children, rather than adult professional dancers.

After the girls left with Rashmi's mother, Divya stayed back there for a while, hoping that the new housekeeper would materialize on the other side of Shalini's boundary wall. She wanted to strike up an acquaintance with her -

to find out as much as possible about that mysterious house with its secretive tenant. Only after that would she reveal her apprehensions, which, for all she knew, could be unfounded, to Divya.  But though she hung around for twenty minutes or more, there was no sign of that woman. So, she retraced her steps, heading back to IIMK, knowing that it was no point waiting for Shalini - who would want to spend as much time as possible with an ailing friend - to turn up.

# XIV

When Mohan walked into the room of his friend and fellow-conspirator Sekhar, the man was sitting with a glum face.

'Why so sour', Mohan asked, lighting up a cigarette.

'It's that idiot, Ashok', Sekhar said angrily. 'He has bungled up placement work. You know he is one of the student reps in the placement committee. That stingy paisa counter Navaneetham has recommended a fine of Rs. 25,000 on him and is taking it up with the director and the program committee'.

'Dud! Jackass!', Mohan gave his opinion of their student friend. 'But you are his personal faculty adviser appointed by the director and have to bear the burden of his sins'.

'No, not appointed by the director; only a temporary allocation by the program committee'.

'Whatever. Anyhow, it is good you are his counselor. As your friend, I can order him about, make him run errands'.

In saying so, Mohan was not exaggerating. In some institutions–thought not at IIMs–Ph.D. students had to first report to their adviser's wife in the morning to take purchase orders for fish and vegetables for the day.

"So, I gave him an errand last week', Mohan added.

'Really? What kind of errand?'

'It has to do with the information he gave me, about a 'Swiggy' deliveryman roaming about the campus, near student residences. Remember, we told that to the director, and she took it seriously too'.

'But, Mohan, why should we worry about it? Let the director handle it. We have our affairs to take care of '.

'All right, all right', Mohan said with a touch of irritation. 'But this is our territory, always remember that. Directors come and go, but we are here till the end of our lives. Nothing that goes on here should…..', he paused, searching for the right word in his limited vocabulary, ' should escape us'.

'Fair enough, I see your point. You mentioned the drug mafia to the director. But are we personally concerned?'

'No. let the worthless, spoiled IIMK students get addicted. Who cares!'

Mohan broke off with a string of expletives, startling his more laid-back friend. Some professors at IIMs have a fundamental dislike for their business school students, but stemming only from an academic's aversion to pure profit-oriented activities and the measurement of success based on salaries offered. But Mohan's hatred for these management students was more like murderous class hatred.

'These spoiled brats should be sent as in China and Cambodia to work on farms and cleaning railway station toilets', Mohan screamed and his friend, terrified, looked around to see if they were being overheard.  It also occurred to Sekhar that his friend's broken English seemed to get mended a bit when he lost his temper. Some hidden reserves opening up in the force of his emotions!

Mohan regained control of himself, continuing in a milder voice. 'So, as I was saying, this boy Ashok told me that he had seen this helmeted man walking around student residences, even peering in through backside windows, etc'.

'He could have accosted him on the spot. Why didn't he do that?'

'Nothing solid to go on. He has a permit to deliver food and is allowed in by our guards. A free multi-entry pass! Also, other students and even faculty members will interfere if he questions the man here on campus. Not even the delivery firm will cooperate. I called them up, and they said that they have so many delivery boys, switching areas frequently too, so it is impossible to keep track of them. But,' he stopped frowning, 'I smelt a rat. It was almost as if they were saying what they were told to say'.

'Well, could be. We know the drug mafia is very powerful, financially as well'.

'So, I thought we could get some information on our initiative. I told Ashok to trail the man next time he sees him. That is, the next time he comes and leaves, making sure it is the same man under the helmet. We can at least find out where he comes from'.

'I see, follow him to his lair', Sekhar nodded understandingly. Then we could also see what assorted drug packages he stores there for delivery'

Mohan frowned again. 'I have a sixth-sense feeling that he is not what he makes himself out to be'.

'Of course, you have. That is why you gave your jackass

the errand, right? But let us not be unfair to him. He might have succeeded in his errand. Oh, good, here he comes!'

Ashok stepped into the room with a sheepish look. It was Mohan who started the interrogation.

'Well?'

'Oh, about this food delivery fellow....', Ashok mumbled, scratching his head. 'It didn't go so well'.

'Jackass', Mohan muttered.

Pretending not to have heard the 'compliment', Ashok continued.

'When he left campus, he had four of behind him, a good distance away. Three boys and a girl, all first-years who look up to me, I may say'.

Mohan grunted and said impatiently, 'Go on'.

'The bike rider went off towards   the National Institute of Technology, keeping to the main bus route itself. Then I got a feeling that he was leading us on a wild goose chase, knowing that we were behind him'.

'That was clear from the beginning', Mohan said softly, 'he must have noticed you right at our gate'.

Ashok winced but continued. 'So, I formed a strategy. Seeing a narrow bridge long ahead, I told two of the students to overtake him and turn around at the bridge to cut him off. We could then hem in him from behind, then question him. Nobody would interfere as they would on campus'.

'Sounds good, but did it work?', Sekhar asked even as Mohan shook his head.

'No', Ashok said in a low voice. 'It's not clear what happened. The two students got ahead to the bridge. Bu then a good van came from somewhere, cutting across the road diagonally, blocking our view. When it had passed the bike- rider was not to be seen. He was not on the road ahead of the bridge, and not before the bridge'.

'Under the bridge, then', Mohan said with a sardonic laugh.

'You are so right sir', Ashok said, but Mohan didn't look flattered. 'We then discovered a very narrow mud path leading down to the riverside, through the shadow of a large tree, so that it is not readily noticed. That was the route he must have taken. We drove down ourselves, but there was no sign of him.  Many small paths break off towards houses on the riverfront; he could have taken any of those'.

'Well-done', Mohan said sarcastically. Ashok pretended to be looking down at the mobile in his hand.

'No harm was done', Mohan added in a conciliatory tone. 'He will be back and we will get the information we want. If what he is up to doesn't affect us, we need not take any action. We are not the local guardians of these puffed-up kids, are we? But if he is playing the same game as us....'

Sekhar quickly broke in, again looking around to see if anyone was around. 'So, Ashok, tell us about your placement debacle'.

'It's this puffed-up faculty member Navaneethem who has messed up everything', Ashok said in a complaining tone, using the term Mohan had picked to refer to the students he disliked. 'He has unnecessarily kicked up a row'.

Ashok paused, drawing a long breath before launching into a long narrative he would slant as he wished to make his actions look innocent and well-motivated.

# XV

Navaneetham has been picked for the post of Chairman, Placements, by Sujata herself after she came to IIMK, a post that is held normally for two full academic years. Though he took up the post in June, the active placement season started only a few weeks before the Christmas -New Year break, during which many students like Divya chose to stay back on campus–rather than go home–to finish term papers which were due only when the new term started in January.

Sujata had chosen him for the post for a specific reason: he was known to be a stickler for procedures and formalities, a reputation he garnered from the way he handled regular classes. Such a mindset, though rather repelling when manifested in all its strength, would be useful, even necessary when handling the placement process which could go haywire at any juncture. It would not be an exaggeration to say that in past years–and under past directors–it had been the law of the jungle that governed placements. True, companies would choose the person best suited for their needs, but the question was who would be produced before them to be chosen from. Brute force akin to someone pushing aside an old lady to get into a bus firstand wily manipulations was the name of the game in placement.

To his credit, Navaneetham came down hard on that ruthless game. None who had observed him during his regular lectures would have been surprised, but they would have said that he went too far, that some boys and girls who were subjected to his disciplinary actions may have become traumatized. So, his zero-tolerance policy towards discipline and code of behavior in the class had several critics among the faculty group itself.

At a faculty get-together at tea time, Malavika, a recruit to the organizational behavior area, smiled somewhat impishly at Navaneetham and said,

'I heard that you gave real hiding to that girl Kanchana during your lecture last week'.

Malavika was in her late twenties and had been hired at the assistant professor's level. Lulled to complacency by her perfectly round face projecting baby-like innocence, people were often taken aback later when exposed to the beam of her quicksilver mind. Dressed in a bright kurta-pajama combination, she leaned sideways to look straight into the eyes of Navaneetham.

'Hiding?' How ridiculous! What on earth do you mean?', Navaneetham pretended that he had no idea of what Malavika was talking about.

'I take that back', Malavika conceded generously. 'Not hiding in the literal sense of the word. But, perhaps equally potent, a verbal thrashing that made that girl burst into tears'.

She paused for a moment, hesitating, seeing Navaneetham's battle-ready expression, but then added:

'What did she actually do to merit that? I mean the

scolding'.

Navaneetham looked around furtively and noticing that several other faculty members were listening, simmered down. Adopting a casual, matter-of-fact tone, he addressed Malavika.

'This was not the first time that she had misbehaved in class. I would be in the middle of some extremely important delivery, the key to discussion for the rest of the period when this girl would lapse into loud chatter'.

'Chatter, Chattering?', Malavika asked, uncomprehending. 'You mean, on her mobile phone?'

'No', Navaneetham's voice turned a bit shrill, 'chatting with a boy sitting a few seats away. Mind you, no whispering to the person in the very next seat, that wouldn't disturb me. Rather, loud conversation with someone sitting a good distance away'.

Malavika was going to ask what the students had been talking about, but Rakesh broke in:

'But, dear Navaneetham, did you find out what they had been talking about?'

'Definitely not about what was being discussed in class right then, I can assure you that', Navaneetham said with conviction.

'No, true enough, but only partially. You see, she was praising you!', Rakesh said smiling. 'Listen, Navaneetham, I was there at the coffee-vending machine when the girl came there crying, leaning on her friends; must have been during break-time in your lecture. I found out what had happened'.

"Well, I told you just now what had happened'.

'Not quite', Rakesh lifted a hand to silence his intransigent colleague. 'She had leaned over to tell her friend that your lecture was superb, that you make a dry subject so interesting with the way you deliver!'

'I didn't know, had no idea…..', Navaneetham stuttered, mollified – but also flattered, and fell silent. Then he added in a low voice, 'she could have told that straight to me'.

'What!  Could she have stood up in class just to say your lecture is interesting?', Malavika gave a dry laugh. 'Actually, I like it when students chit-chat in my class. Shows they are astutely following what is going on, not just sitting and day-dreaming. I think they mostly chat about the contents of what is being said by the professor'.

Then she added, quite unexpectedly, causing many an eyebrow to be raised around: 'geniuses, most of them, I think, our students.

'I wouldn't say that I really wouldn't', Mitra interposed. 'Perhaps they think they are geniuses, but that is a wholly different matter'.

'Dr. Mitra is right', said Navaneetham, coming back to life, relieved that the particular episode of a teacher humiliating his admirer was no longer the topic of conversation. 'They think they are CEOs also already. Why I was once laying out a statistical test and this idiot sitting in the front row asks me if the test is of any use to him after graduation. As a CEO, he said, the results of the test will be laid at his table, so why should he study the procedure of the test - he had the cheek to ask. Such arrogance, don't you agree with me?'

'One visiting finance faculty member was once telling

me', Mitra said, voicing support for Navaneetham's view of student attitudes, 'that the students taking his course think that they are going to be working with mergers and take-overs as soon as they get their first jobs. These kids, he said, are not prepared to do any nitty-gritty groundwork in finance or accounting, which is what they will be asked to do'.

'So what our IIMK graduates do is to leave the first job and hop over to the next job within six months', Navaneetham said drily. 'No wonder some companies have a policy of not hiring from IIMs. They only go to the second-tier group of management schools – and are happy with the performance of the boys and girls they pick up at those institutions'.

'But do you think that the people who come to interview for their companies are that easily hoodwinked?'. Malavika sounded skeptical about the broad sweeps on the canvas made by her colleague.

'They are usually human behavior specialists and can look into the minds of our students. I believe that if you observe closely, you will see that they are hiring those students who will fit into their company environment and hierarchies. They are not out to get the highest grade-taker who will hop on to another company wagon at the first opportunity'.

'Malavika is right', Rakesh nodded. 'Just see who got the highest offer last year. The kid was a graduate of some unknown army college in some God-forsaken place and had only a 'B' average. But he landed the highest offer of 30 lakhs. Why, because he was a personable kid with a go-go nature, always ready with a smile, never showing stress-related behavior or symptoms when under stress, even during stress-interviewing'.

'I have not met this boy you are talking about, Rakesh since he graduated before I joined', Malavika said. 'But I would guess that he was very good in group activities also, as a good percentage of IIMK students. It is as if they perform above their capability limits when put into a group. And the output of the group itself becomes more than the sum of the individual outputs: the group's energy level exceeds the sum of the members' energy levels'.

'Unfortunately, the students work well in group activities with their seniors too', Mitra said in a sarcastic tone.

'I don't understand', Malavika frowned.

'I had a term paper for my course, several topics to choose from for the students. Never mind what the topics were, but perhaps I made a mistake in including topics given to the current senior students. Guess what, I found that one boy had copied ditto from the previous year's term paper of one of his senior students. Soul mates, the two of them, obviously. Good group work isn't it, looking at the sum of the group output summed over years!'

Malavika started to say something but restrained herself.

'Did this happen this year?', Navaneetham asked, sounding pleased, obviously happy to... in a pleasing voice, obviously happy to linger on the topic that vindicated his tough stance towards students.

'No. Last year. I made the bot stay back after convocation to finish the term paper. He lost three months–

and also the job he picked up at placements. The director had approved the action taken, said it will serve as an example to discourage academic malpractices'.

'Well-done, Mitra', Navaneetham applauded with raised hands.

But Mitra was unrelenting, had not exhausted his vituperative volley on the behavioural patterns of IIM students. 'What I am saying is that', he added, looking directly at Malavika, 'it may be true that our students interact well with each other in a group, but there their soft skills end, it is not transferrable outside their little group. You cannot repudiate the fact that they have a superior air, consider themselves to be a cut above second-tier MBA school graduates'.

'And also a cut above their teachers at IIMK', Navaneethem hastened to supplement the charges being made.

Malavika laughed out aloud.

'you know why, Navaneetham', she said between bouts of laughter, 'that is simply because they get much higher salaries than us when they graduate, not because they feel they are better at your subject and can give superior lectures. They walk out of here with salaries four times our own. But we should be happy about this state of affairs, shouldn't we? Our students being received so well in the competitive dog-eat-dog corporate world ought to be a matter of pride for us'.

'Matter of pride, my foot! Mitra exploded. 'Our peanut salary is a matter of eternal shame. Unfortunately, these arrogant kids think we are stuck here at low salaries because we cannot compete in the corporate job market'.

'Well, we made the choice ourselves, didn't we', Rakesh shrugged his shoulders as if to say it is so obvious. 'Taking a Ph.D. is a definite choice to step into the academic world– where the rewards and merits are not measured in monetary terms. Remember the story about Einstein's first job in the U.S? The Institute of Advanced Studies in Princeton offered him a position when the War broke out, asking him what salary would be appropriate to him.  He mentioned such a ridiculously low figure that they wrote back telling him not to bother, that he couldn't live on that and that they will take care of the matter.  So, you see, in this academic world of ours, we get satisfaction from sources other than income'.

'Creativity, publishing articles....', Malavika mused.

'Of course, a Ph.D. does not necessarily rule you out from the corporate world', Rakesh pointed out, 'at least, not from consulting'.

'You may be right, Rakesh sir', Jose who had been having tea at the adjacent table said, joining the lengthy debate going on.  A stranger wearing a visitor's badge around the neck was beside with him. Rakesh thought he had seen that man with Jose earlier too. Jose didn't bother to introduce the visitor, seemed eager to make his point:

'But an MBA is better for consulting, isn't it so? Some of our students get consulting jobs with McKinsey and other such companies. Some have even started consulting firms, Dr. Rakesh. But not always that successful, unfortunately' Jose added with a grin. 'A few years back we had a student, Shakuntala, who had always publicly stated that she would start her consulting firm'.

'And did she do that finally?', Rakesh asked, looking with curiosity at the stranger in Jose's company. He now remembered that he had seen him around many times - at the lunch and tea tables, but also in various other parts of the campus. Must be a building contractor or a Kerala Water Authority official, Rakesh surmised.

'Things looked all set for her', Jose answered. 'But then an unfortunate incident occurred. Shakuntala had an old scooter, second-hand, or third-hand, or even fourth hand, purchased from the agent who buys bikes from departing IIMK students at throwaway prices. She loved riding around on it, shopping, even going up to the city centre: but, mark, without a license'.

'Smart girl!', Malavika gave her judgement.

Jose stopped, surprised, but continued. 'Perhaps not so smart, Dr. Malavika. One day she ran plumb into an old lady who was half-heartedly trying to cross the road, moving forward and backwards. The lady was not seriously hurt, but it became a police case. It would have become a major blow to IIMK's reputation, but the director hushed it up. The bike was given to the old lady, whose grandson uses it now'. Jose smiled. 'And, by the way, that boy is only sixteen and does not have a license either!'

'I say, that's an interesting tale, Jose', Rakesh laughed. 'But did the girl finally achieve her dream of starting a consultancy'.

'Yes, of course. She invited the director for the installation ceremony, but he threw the invitation into the wastepaper basket'.

'Awful! MCP!', Malavika said angrily.

'Beg your pardon, MCP?'. Then Jose saw Rakesh wink at him and didn't pursue the 'enquiry'. 'And, he said, who will ever consult that girl!'.

Malavika stirred her teacup so vigorously that half the tea spilled over.

'That's unfair', Rakesh said decisively. 'Failure in one walk of life does not rule out success in other areas. In college, I had a friend who I thought was definitely potty. Once I was riding behind him on his bike when it starts raining heavily. To my surprise, he started going very fast. I cried out at him to slow down, but he shouted back, "I can't see anything through my specs, have to reach the hostel as fast as possible". So, I could be excused for slotting him into a low IQ category; his grades were nothing much to wrote home either'.

'I understand', Jose said, 'he has done well in life, hasn't he, Dr. Rakesh'.

'I suppose one could say so', Rakesh said, looking earnestly at Navaneetham for some reason. Navaneetham shifted uncomfortably in his seat. 'He is among the top fifty CEOs in the country now'.

'Success for risk-takers, fools barge in where angels fear to tread', Malavika murmured.

'All this talk is fine', Navaneetham said in a complaining voice. 'Where do we have consulting at IIMK? We know that faculty at the older IIMs, A, B, and C, get an enormous amount of consulting assignments. What I have heard is that the earlier directors had deliberately followed a policy of squashing consulting by faculty members, to get them to teach more. You know, firms usually approach the director with queries about consulting; so, if the director wishes to do so, he can scotch the possibilities in the bud itself'.

'Yes, I have heard this too, though I am new here', Malavika conceded. 'But I also heard that the directors had a good reason to do so, to discourage consulting. Faculty shortage was a perennial problem. You see, recruits from other states tended to resign and leave soon as their spouses could not find jobs in this small town. I heard about the wife of a professor from Punjab who had to take up a nursery teacher's job though she had been a college professor back home. So, probably, the first directors had to burden the faculty members very heavily. This meant no consulting and also teaching in non-specialized areas. There is also this story about an operations area man who was asked to teach OB!'

'Must have been tough times, the beginning years', Rakesh mused. Then he said aloud, 'Just imagine having to function from temporary premises, under the administrative control–to some extent at least - of another institution. I believe the IIMK administrative section and the classrooms were in a part of the REC–now called NIT, Calicut–complex, while the faculty rooms were in the government computer organization CEDT's complex.

When the time came for their lectures'.the faculty members were driven down to the classrooms which were a kilometer away.

'But, Dr. Rakesh, if you will excuse me', Jose broke in apologetically, 'I must say that we received tremendous support from the - then - REC director, Prof. Chandrasekharan'.

'Of course, I have heard that too', Rakesh nodded.

'How he would be in the front row on the MBA programme inauguration day, all ears to note any complaints and suggestions, especially from the senior students who were given the floor on that occasion to express their sentiments to the people at the very top'.

'I believe that the first batch of IIMK faculty members was given buckets, to go and fetch water', Mitra said vaguely, as if to throw a bucket of cold water on the warm sentiments bubbling up.

'No, not really', said Rakesh, laughing. 'That's just stories - though it may have been the case that faculty accommodation was not up to the mark till the REC International House was placed at IIMK's disposal'.

'Tell me, Navaneetham', Rakesh said, changing the subject of the conversation, which he felt was slipping away towards pure gossip, 'what's this I hear about you imposing a stiff fine for malpractice in placement activities? The placement season has started in earnest, right?'

'So you are using brass knuckles in placement also, Dr. Navaneetham, not just in classes?', Malavika couldn't help adding a malicious comment.

Navaneetham looked uncomfortable. He had already been criticized for imposing penalties at too high levels relative to the misdemeanours of students. The most recent such episode occurred when he functioned on the committee for the selection of the best all-rounder student. In the very first meeting of the committee, he deleted the name of a student on the shortlist. 'But, why, Dr., Navaneetham, the boy has a high GPA, and a record of contributions on all extra-curricular activities, including social service projects, arranging inter-institutional meets and all that'. Navaneetham contended strongly that the boy had bad manners and poor social interaction, giving the boy's behavior during his lecture as an example:

'I would have started the lecture, but this fellow would stand up, his back to me, mind you, his back turned towards me, talking to someone in the row behind him'.

'But, Dr. Navaneetham', the other committee members had pleaded, 'is that such a serious offence'. But to no avail; Navaneetham was unrelenting, had used his veto power to throw the 'bad-mannered boy' out of the running for the best all-rounder student.

That extreme step he had taken had also established at one stroke Navaneetham's reputation as a hard, unforgiving taskmaster–who would only flit about in the upper range of possible penalties to be imposed. It is possible that Sujata had not been fully aware of his reputation in this respect when giving him the placement chairperson's post. But, on the other hand, she had been also looking for a tough hand to manage the notoriously fickle placement processes.

'Don't exaggerate now, Malavika', Navaneetham lifted one finger in a reprimanding gesture. 'I never had brass knuckles on, even in classes. This boy Ashok in the Placement Committee set a record in manipulation for own, totally selfish ends'.

'What is there to manipulate in Placements?', Rakesh asked, feigning innocence.

'You will be aghast at the possibilities, Rakesh! There are possibilities in plenty for scheming minds'.

'Like what, can you elaborate a little?'

'For the highly rated companies, students with the

highest GPAs get the first places in the interview list. So, the best students have the first go. Only if they do not get selected do the students with lower GPAs, it could be just half a grade average less, get called for these interviews with the top firms'.

'I am getting an inkling about the possibilities you mentioned', Malavika said slowly. 'So, did this boy Ashok jump the queue unfairly, perhaps giving a false GPA?'

'That would have been too obvious, he's cleverer than that. But what he did was worse than that. He upgraded his grade average unilaterally, with his method, without asking anyone, not me, not the other student and faculty members in the committee'.

'But, Navaneetham, this is impossible, inconceivable', Rakesh sounded incredulous. 'The grades are there in black and white for everybody to see'.

'True, but wait till you hear to what extent that devious mind sank! Ashok reckons that he has technically three years of work experience, as an apprentice in his father's family firm. Let me clarify that here at IIMK (and other IIMs as well), we do not count that as work experience during the process of student selection. But just see what this crooked mastermind did. He counted his three years as valid work experience and made up an arbitrary rule that GPAs can be upgraded taking into account the years of work experience'.

'Utter nonsense', Rakesh said, still looking amazed. 'And, what a fool he is! How can he makeup such a contorted rule based on false premises and expect people to accept it?'

'No, no, he didn't expect anyone to accept the rule. He probably thought he could write up his GPA and that other students will not be aware of what is happening, trusting him as a committee member. The arbitrary rule was only something to fall back upon if someone raised a question about his grade appreciation'.

'Then who found it out, the anomaly?'

'Elizabeth, the other student representative in the Placement Committee. She was not involved in grade comparison or checking, that was Ashok's responsibility. She just happened to check the GPAs one day, that is all'.

'Well, she's a smart girl', Mitra commented unexpectedly. He was not one to praise anybody–for anything. So, there were some raised eyebrows around the table. 'She must have realized that something was seriously wrong with this jerk's high placing in the list'.

'Could be', Navaneetham threw open his palms as if seeking support, even approbation. 'So, what else could I have done? The disciplinary action for such a case of malpractice in a committee is not clear, not there in any manual!'

'You could always strike him off the best all-rounders' list', Malavika said in an undertone.

Navaneetham winced but pretended he had not felt Malavika's barb.

'You cannot dismiss a student from the programme for such an action', he said, laying out the grounds for the defense of his choice of penalty. 'Nor can you throw him out of the student residence. Placement is unrelated to housing; he should have misbehaved in some manner in the hostel to earn such a penalty. So, I thought I would pinch him where it would hurt him most, financially. He has a reputation for being a miser, free-riding when students give parties, not chipping in to share the bill when dining out with friends, and so on. So, a 25,000 Rupee fine for such a crooked miser felt just right for me'.

'Not a bad idea really', Malavika conceded–and that was music for Navaneetham's ears, coming from such a person who, he felt, was in the habit of baiting him. 'But did Dr. Sujata give the green signal?'

'Yes', Navaneetham said, now quite upbeat. 'She said she couldn't think of any alternate action'.

'Probably, she didn't (didn't have much of a choice) have a choice', Rakesh suggested, 'in these days of the right to information, any penalties given to students can fall under the microscope. So, dismissals or asking a student to come back for the next batch etc. can put the director in the dock'.

'And how are placements going anyway', Malavika asked as the tea group started dispersing.

'Not bad at all, not bad at all', Navaneetham beamed. 'We blew away existing records in offer money the very first day'.

Rakesh gave a thumbs-up sign while Malavika rolled her eyes upwards as if to indicate that there are more important things in life and at IIMK.

The version of the placement fiasco that Ashok presented to his official and unofficial mentor differed– as could be imagined – greatly from that of his indignant placement committee faculty colleague.

'I did not supersede anyone against the rules', he bleated pitifully. 'The students who had higher GPAs had been also called for two-three other top-notch, premium interviews. Thus, they naturally forfeited their right to appear for the interview for which I was therefore upgraded to'.

'I don't understand', his faculty adviser Sekhar frowned. 'What is that fellow Navaneetham screaming about then? How could he, if what you say is true, impose a hefty fine on you?'

Surprisingly, Ashok's unofficial mentor, Mohan, came out to support his protégé–whom he had ridiculed just a few minutes ago.

'Oh, that Navaneetham is a strange fellow. Off his rocker, if you ask me. Also, stuck up, nose in the air just like the students he despises; a useless idiot. No reason for us to accept his version against Ashok's'.

Sekhar guessed the reason for his friend's turnaround. Mohan was just not interested in any activity that did not concern him or his goals – add, his manipulations - and didn't want to waste time discussing such matters.

Still, Sekhar did not back off at once.

"But, Ashok, tell me then, why did Elizabeth, the other student representative in the committee, become a signatory to the charges leveled against you?'

Ashok was ready with his prepared answer.

'Sir, we have to understand that Elizabeth is totally under Navaneetham's thumb. Not only is he her faculty adviser, but he is also handling all the electives she had taken this term. So, sir, can we expect her to oppose him on this or any other matter, even if it is the breakfast menu at the canteen?'

'All right, Ashok, no harm done. You can afford that 25,000. Pay it and get back into the placement list, they haven't banished you. You are sure to get a good offer'.

'Even a monkey will get an offer if it is wearing an IIMK t-shirt', Mohan thought, but desisted from saying that aloud. He was happy that the issue had been sorted out without an open tussle with Navaneetham. He had better use for Ashok than on such 'trivialities'.

'Good, Sekhar', he said aloud approvingly. 'Let's not waste time discussing placement prospects for these arrogant kids. They will get their high offers, work from dawn to midnight on stupid jobs. The stress will drive them into drink and drugs and they will fall early into their graves'.

Mohan lifted his eyebrows questioningly at Sekhar:

'And we don't care, do we?'

# XVI

When Divya turned into Shalini's flower-lined path towards the porch, she was pleased to see a three-wheeler auto-rickshaw parked to the side there. So, I am plumb on time, she congratulated herself but wondered why a three-wheeler was chosen for the city trip, not a regular taxi.

Even a bus ride would have been fine since buses in Calicut usually keep time and a good pace too.

The door opened at the very first ring. 'Come in and have some jackfruit chips', Shalini took her hand and led her inside with a broad smile. She was dressed in non-Kerala style, in a bright kurta-pyjama combination that set off her dancer's figure to advantage.

'We are made for each other', Divya said laughing, as she was also sporting a similar combination. Anyone seeing them together would have taken them to be sisters, the age difference hardly obvious.

They sat down at a small table by the living room window that faced the IIM neighbour's house.

'Hope you didn't have to cancel dancing tuition to function as my tourist guide this evening'. Divya had been feeling guilty on that score, as she knew that Shalini stuck meticulously to schedules to be able to fulfill all her diverse commitments.

'No, you don't have to feel bad, Divya! Today is not a dance tuition day'.

'That reminds me', Divya said with some excitement in her voice. 'Have you sounded the parents of your little students? I am asking because Rakesh and Roshan, who are involved in the organization of the IIMK international conference, have given the green signal for your troupe's performance on the final day'.

'Yes, and they have agreed too, are, in fact, rather proud about the demand in high echelons for their children's little dancing feet!

She leaned over and touched Divya's hand lightly. 'And, guess what the kids said? They told me in one voice that they will come and perform only if Divya chechi is there!  I thought that was sweet of them'.

'Yes, indeed, how rare of them!  Though, probably it is only because my dull familiar face will make them feel secure in a strange place! But no big deal, I am going to be there. Rakesh told me specifically that I should be at the Taj for the concluding day's activities, as I am the contact person for your group'.

'I can see that you love these kids, Divya', Shalini said softly, 'even though you have been with them only for a relatively short while. I think it is because you are a child yourself'.

Divya pretended to be indignant. 'What, do you feel I am childish?'

Shalini laughed. 'I think you know what I mean. I mean

that you have a child's innocence, nice quality in an adult'.

'Shalini, I will be there watching over these children like a hawk. I think I will die of shock if anything happens to any of these children'.

'I know, I know. I remember how distressed you were when that girl Tanya fell off her dad's bike and broke her wrist. Still, I am discounting your exaggerated statement a bit: to use language a business student is at home with'.

'At this rate, you will tell me one day that my net present value to you is negative', Shalini retorted, then held up her hand demanding silence.

A nightingale had started singing, softly at first, then raising its tone steadily, insistently.

'How sweet! Diya cried. Is it here often by your house? I hear a nightingale sometimes from the student residence, but rarely, very infrequently'.

'This one is always around; I can hear it sing every day. And, I found out to my great joy that it is one of a pair. That's uncommon, seeing nightingale in pairs'.

'True', Divya nodded. On the other hand, the common bird around here, the brown and yellow birds, mynah, always appears in pairs'.

'Let me tell you, it is considered bad luck around here if you see a single mynah. But if you have seen only one and are fearing that bad luck will strike, the other one always appears from somewhere'.

'Did you ever see this nightingale? It must be always hidden among the leaves being a shy, secretive bird - though it pulls the plugs when singing'.

'Oh yes, I have seen it a couple of times. As you say, it is hidden among the leaves of that mango tree right at the edge of my house grounds. But if you go to that corner, where my boundary wall against the IIMK professor's house meets my backside wall, you can catch sight of it. Try that sometimes. But for heaven's sake, don't turn around there and look at the backside of that house; the curtains are always open there and it will seem as if you are spying on them–or are a peeping Tom!'.

'I will think about it' Divya said as if asking her not to peep is a violation of her fundamental rights. Anyhow, I am not going to do it now–I mean watch the nightingale. I will keep that experience for my next visit if the bird is then willing to reveal its gracious self on that occasion!  We got to be leaving now if we are going to be able to do any sightseeing, right?'

The auto driver was patiently waiting, reading the local newspaper which he put away with a glad smile. He must have waited for a longer time than he had bargained for, Shalini thought, feeling a bit guilty.

'Side shutters up or down madam', he asked briskly in an exaggerated professional manner.

'Up of course', Shalini said with a touch of irritation. 'It's not raining, is it?'

Looking abashed, the auto driver leaped on to his seat and took off at a sedate pace.

'Side shutters down indeed!', Shalini leaned over and whispered to Divya. 'I am taking the auto because we get so much cool breeze from all directions; it is less enclosed than a regular taxi. One gets a better view too, towards all sides'.

'It was an excellent idea on your part,'Divya agreed. 'I have also heard a lot about the honesty and integrity of Calicut auto drivers'.

'You can say that again', Shalini said animatedly. 'Every outsider who comes here has noted that. There was a national basketball championship in Calicut last year. The delegates from other states were at first wary of taking autos, fearing they would be fleeced. But then, after they have experimented once, they took autos for all trips, even for distances of a few hundred meters. The auto driver took only the exact meter charge from them, returning even 50 paise: an eye-opener for the sportsmen and women from other states!'

'Roshan says the buses here are fine too, but I have never taken a bus ride in Calicut'.

'True enough, but then you got to know the system here, and also be nimble on your feet. A certain degree of athletic ability is required. The bus has a conductor, called 'kili (bird)' in Malalyalam, who calls all the shots. He can often help you get off the bus by giving you a push as you stand delicately poised on the step of the exit door. A foreign lady had come to watch my dance classes once from the city, and this happened: the 'kili' gave her a helpful push to get off'.

'But that was good, wasn't it? I mean, she might have missed the stop, unable to get off'.

'You think so? A nice push to help her get off and there the foreign woman lay on the road. Fortunately, not flat on her face, but on all fours'

'Terrible! I see your point about being familiar with the

system. True, all over the world, I would imagine. Anyway, I don't think I will risk an encounter with any 'kili' on any bus!'

Both of them laughed, the wind blowing their hair across their faces. Divya started singing softly:

'On a desert highway

 Cool wind in my hair…'

'Come off it Divya', Shalini gasped. 'You are not headed to Hotel California, and this is no desert highway. Just look at the coconut and mango groves on both sides'.

'Yeh, but this is real nice. Cool wind blowing - from the seaside, I guess. As you said, the auto beats the taxi in this respect, being open on all sides'. She looked over to Shalini's side of the road, leaning across. 'It is, indeed, lush greenery all around even though there are regular rows of houses too. No high-rise buildings, thank goodness'.

'Glad you liked the choice. I have told the driver to take a few detours to show us the wetland areas. Those areas sort of encircle the city, coming in at some points, and you can reach them by side roads from many main city roads and highways'

'That's lovely. You should be seeing a lot of migratory birds in these wetlands'.

'Of course, from very far-away places like Siberia. You know, some of these birds fly huge distances. One such bird, a small-sized one, loves eternal summer and flies some 30,000 km each year to fulfill its wish. In a life span of 26 years, it flies three times the distance to the moon from the earth'.

'Unbelievable! But as in all developing countries, the

process of economic growth must be ringing the death knell for all this'.

'That's right. These wetlands are now in danger from real estate developments. But here a strong wetland protection movement has surfaced. I believe even people from CWRDM, the water management organization behind IIMK, are active in this movement. The problem is that sometimes the wetlands are being taken over by the government itself, now the latest step is to develop a transport hub. The idea is good because the traffic chaos in the city will be reduced. But though the ends are good, should not the means also be evaluated?'

Shalini leaned backwards. 'But no more talk till we reach the city centre. Or else you will miss all the sights and scenery along the way'.

It took about an hour for them to reach the centre of town. The auto was parked in a parking lot and they walked towards Mananchira square with its large tank and nearby park.

Divya shook her head. 'The IIMK students only go to the Taj and other pubs and the beach. I don't think any of us have explored these areas'.

'I believe the ruling dynasty kings, the Samudiris, had their military garrisons in this area' Shalini said. 'You may not know this: while the dynasty was Hindu, the military commanders were always Muslims, from the Marakkar family'.

'How awesome! Shows the remarkable communal amity existing those days, doesn't it?'

'Arabs used to come here from very ancient times,

even before they accepted Islam. Many of them married local women and settled down. In the large market called "Valiyangadi", many foreign tongues could be heard'

'I have heard that about Kochi too', Diya said, 'that many foreign languages could be heard in markets and drinking places. Like Calicut, it too was active in trade, isn't it? This vacation Roshan had gone to the old trading village Muziris which had trade with the Roman empire- and even with King Solomon's Jerusalem. The Chinese were in Kochi too, left their legacy in fishing nets. What a round sea journey they must have undertaken!'

'I have heard that Solomons' ships docked at 'Ophir', further down the coast', Shalini said doubtfully. 'But perhaps they came to Muziris too. And, by the way, the Chinese did not ignore Calicut. I saw an issue of The Times magazine which had a section on sea explorations before Vasco de Gama and other Europeans. Chinese explorers and emissaries were in Calicut and reported back to the Emperor that it was a great country that had seen, with a happy and prosperous population'.

'Obviously, it was the trade that brought prosperity to Calicut of that age', Divya, who was a steadfast proponent of reducing barriers to trade, opined. Then she repeated the statement, loudly, as if totally convinced about the point being made.

Divya loved S.M Street, popularly known as 'Mittayi' or 'sweets' street. Few wouldn't. Street vendors called out to her waving colourful dresses, shouting out their bargains. She wasn't the only one enjoying the spectacle. Talking of Arabs, an Arab family passed by, two elderly men beaming broadly with pleasure, and the ladies in tow laughing, stepping around young vendors who accosted them at near quarters with dresses and bracelets at bargain prices.

'The statue at the beginning of the street is that of a famous writer from these parts called S.K. Pottekad', Shalini informed her young friend. He has even written a book on the pulsating life and lives on this street called 'The story of a street'. She pointed to the shops lining the street. 'A lot is going on inside there, but don't expect to be able to bargain— which tourists love doing as it gives them a thrill. Most of the owners of these shops run their business as a lifestyle, not purely for profits; they wouldn't know what to do each day if their shops are wound up. So, they fix a reasonable price and do not deviate from that'.

'That's cool really. Will remember that when I go shopping here without you', Divya said, trying not to bump into anyone on the crowded pathway.

'Now that we have had our fill of the sights and sounds of the Sweets Street, let's go and lie down on the grass in the Mananchira grass park', Shalini suggested. 'I have the feeling that you have something important to tell me, but that something is holding you back. We can talk in private there with no disturbances as the vendors are not allowed inside the park'.

The vendors may be banned inside the park, but the ban did not apply to tiny sparrows. As soon as they had thrown themselves down on a cool spot on the grass a bunch of these birds appeared, hopping about.

'Looking for scraps, poor things', Shalini said sadly. "Their numbers have come down drastically. Just some years back you would be standing on the railway platform, and these birds will be all over the place, pecking around'.

"I suppose it has to do with indiscriminate cutting down of trees', Divya said.

'Well, that too, but more because our building styles have changed with few roofed structures, which means there are no nesting places for these birds. The new method of packaging grains in plastic has also meant that there are no spill-overs for these birds to pick up at railway platforms and warehouses'.

Divya sighed. 'Progress for human beings is not so good for these poor things'.

'That's putting mildly. It has been inimical for them. Look at the impacts of the mushrooming of mobile towers'.

'Now, unburden your troubles', Shalini said after a while. 'What has been on your mind?'

Divya hesitated a moment and then opened up another front to her friend's disappointment:

'By the way, you haven't told me, what was that lucky charm all about?'

'Oh, I forgot to tell you. That was no lucky charm. It was your friend's, that charming lady's, daughter's horoscope. To be matched with Roshan's!  Evidently, she liked Roshan so much and wanted to strike while the iron was hot when all of you have had a pleasant get-together'.

'This beats everything', Divya shook her head. 'But why didn't she tell me?'

'I think it is standard procedure around these parts: first, match the horoscope before taking any further steps or even discussing it around'.

'Whatever. And do the horoscopes match? I know you

have Roshan's at your fingertips, by heart'.

'Unfortunately, they don't'. Shalini shook her head, but Divya thought she detected a happy undertone and smiled to herself.

'What went wrong? Is there something fundamentally wrong with the girl's horoscope?'

'No, not that.  So-called fundamentally flawed horoscopes can always be matched sensibly. The problem is that these two are born under stars, in the twenty-eight stars in our reckoning, lying three stars away from each other. Such positioning under the stars means that their personalities are incompatible – even though there can be an initial period of euphoria'.

'I don't have the slightest idea of what you are talking about, Shalini'.

'Well, Roshan is born under the star 'Pooram, a good one for men, and that girl on the third star after that, which signals incompatibility. It is just like the Zodiac system. One can see that an Indian and a foreigner born under the same Zodiac sign are much more similar to each other than two Indians born under different Zodiac signs'.

'Fine, you are the best judge in this matter. So, I suppose you will undertake the sad task of disappointing that charming lady'.

'Of course, she will understand if I put it the right way. Anyhow, Roshan seems to have other things on his mind than finding a traditional match in Kerala. He has become very active in making plans for post-IIMK life'.

'Really! Tell me', Divya said enthusiastically. He's become so awfully busy. I hardly get to see him these days.

But', she threw a sideways glance at Shalini, 'it seems he is in regular touch with you always'.

Shalini blushed unaccountably and said hastily, 'he has a couple of start-up projects in mind, has to choose between them. One is to get into the renewable and inexhaustible energy field by investing in windmills. His classmates in the U.S are keen to be partners in the project. The other is the waste management area, which I tell him is better as a social service unless he can come up with new technologies'.

'Sounds good, and I tend to agree with your judgment, Divya said contentedly. 'Roshan has always had very clear goals. Moreover, he draws up short and long-term strategies very elaborately and this minimizes the risk of a manor derailment of any projects'.

'Anyhow, to come back to the not-so-lucky charm package, Roshan is out of the running for your own social development project mate's daughter. Why not consider Rakesh?', Shalini said, throwing a searching glance at her friend.

Divya looked down without answering. Shalini could sense the sadness welling up from her.

'I am sorry, forget it. I was only joking', she said in haste.

'No, you said nothing wrong Shalini, don't feel guilty. Let me come clean. I didn't want to say this, but you ought to know. Moreover, the news will reach your ears, perhaps with wrong connotations even if I don't open up now'. Divya stopped, hesitating again.

'No, no, don't say anything; you don't have to, really, Divya'.

Divya's voice had turned very hoarse suddenly. Shalini could hardly hear her.

'This will shock you. The fact is, Shalini, Rakesh is gay'.

'What!  I don't believe it for a minute. He's built and moves like Kama Deva, the god of love!'

'I agree. Of course, it is not confirmed beyond doubt. I told Roshan to find out if it is true. People may misinterpret if I go around making enquiries. Also', Divya struck a brave note, 'it is not as if Rakesh has anything to hide. Being gay is not a crime anymore in India; section, what is the number now, has been repealed some time back'.

'But how did you get to hear this? Who told you?'

'Nobody told me. I came to know because I overheard a conversation at the lunch table'.

'Go on....'

'I was having lunch with Roshan when the systems manager Mohan came together with a young professor, Sekhar, and sat down at the next table. We were all having our food with little interchange of words when I heard voices being raised. Mohan was saying: "so you see, it is clear. Rakesh is a homo. No wonder we see him moving around with only smart boys. Of course, with exceptions', he added, throwing a look at me.

I didn't react, just sat looking at Roshan, who seemed shaken. But then he turned red with anger, obviously thinking that it is a fabricated tale. This fellow Mohan has a reputation for being sour and nasty and is not popular with either the staff or students'.

'Anyway, it is good that you didn't react then, at the lunch table', Shalini said in a soothing voice. 'Roshan will find out the truth about this rumour'. Then, looking with pity at Divya's sad face, she added, 'and, as you did mention, it is considered normal now in India, as belonging to the private realm; I mean, it is now categorized as someone's private affair that need not concern others'.

'Well, actually I did almost react because Mohan didn't stop there. He again looked sideways at me and said: "and now since being 'gay' is not a crime in India, he can set up a house with that good-looking boy student of his. He may even invite us for the setting up–house ceremony, the palukach, i.e., the milk-boiling ceremony".

I was seeing red and was about to shout at Mohan. But I restrained myself with great difficulty as a man with a guest badge around his neck was sitting at another adjacent table. He was listening to the conversation, though he pretended to be looking at his mobile. Also, at that moment, a foreign visitor came in and joined the group'.

'Which foreigner? Do you mean someone who is registered for the conference? But that is some weeks away'.

'No, he came and sat down with Sekhar. He is a visitor to Sekhar's department, for a whole academic year, I think. So, I couldn't stuff the words back into Mohan's mouth, though I was about to get up from my seat to do that'.

Shalini said nothing, but took her friend's hand and held it as if trying to transfer some positive energy to her. She knew that what had happened was akin to the shattering of a lovely dream for Divya, though the IIMK sojourn for the student is usually all about making it into the best launching pad possible for a quantum leap into the corporate world, a process which has little room or none at all for romantic sentiments.

She deftly changed the subject, sensing a bout of depression beginning to envelop her companion. 'So, as I said, Divya, there is no problem from my side concerning the conference. The parents have agreed to release their kids, are rather proud about it, and the program is also clear: we have picked the items to be performed on stage'.

Divya became attentive again to the surroundings and started discussing some of the practical aspects of the conference.

'We are booking a separate room for you and your group at the Taj that evening. Consider it to be a dressing room, as there is no green room behind the stage. Only thing is, your students will have to walk in their dancing dress and make-up through the regular hotel crowd at the lobby. But they are sure to appreciate the spectacle!'

'It's getting dark' Shalini said, looking around. 'We will keep the temple-type Kuttichira mosque for the next visit: we wouldn't be doing justice to it if we see it half-engulfed in the shadows. If we leave now, we can have an early dinner at my place'.

'We'll keep that also for next time', Divya deferred. 'I think I got to get back to my hostel as early as possible, some things are pending'.

Shalini guessed that her friend was not in the mood for a prolonged stay that evening in anyone's company, even if it was someone emotionally close to her, and so didn't insist.

The auto driver took off with a squealing of tires, at great speed, and maintained that speed, curving in and out of obstructing vehicles. It passed through Shalini's mind that perhaps he too had a dinner appointment, had promised his wife he would be home for an early dinner with a present bought off the evening's income.

At the take-off, Divya lost her balance, falling on to Shalini. Both of them screamed with laughter, and Shalini was hopeful that her companion would be back to her usual cheerful self during the return journey. As the auto sped through the darkness, overtaking regular four-wheeler taxis, Shalini tried to keep up her companion's spirits. The wind was cool and exhilarating, but almost fierce, blowing their hair in all directions. Shalini shouted above the din of the auto-rickshaw:

'You can sing that now, Divya, the highway is dark:

"On a desert highway, cool wind in my hair"

Never mind that it is still coconut palms on either side and you are only headed to IIMK'.

But Divya, though she lifted her face to the wind, only gave a half-grunt in answer.

'This is dangerous', Shalini told herself. 'Such great swings in her moods. She is far more sensitive and vulnerable than I had ever imagined her to be - despite the bold front that she puts up'.

# XVII

Divya did not attend the conference sessions held at IIMK. Some senior students could do that since the final term–during which placement activities loomed most important - was not tightly packed with coursework like the earlier terms. However, Divya did get a detailed and spicy description of the most interesting conference sessions from Roshan and Rakesh who were in the conference organizing committee.

Perhaps it was Sujata's inaugural speech that impressed Divya most. Sujata had been very appreciative of the work that Rakesh had put in, cooperating with one of the board members of the Athenian Management Society (AMS), to make the conference a reality. While most of the foreign delegates were Greeks, there were also a few from the rest of Europe and North America. Rakesh had also tried hard to attract delegates from the well-regarded institutions in India so that the number of delegates had crossed the half-century mark.

'Intellectual interaction between Greek and India goes back to the time Greeks made the first-ever images of The Buddha', Sujata said, smiling at the Greek professor sitting in the front row, Rakesh's collaborator.

'In fact', Sujata continued, 'Aristotle is said to have told Alexander to bring back an Indian teacher when his famous pupil set out to conquer the known world. When Alexander reached the land of the five rivers, Punjab in northwest India, around 300 B.C., the columns of the Maurya Empire, India's first large –scale state formation, were being erected. If the world-conqueror had proceeded deeper into India, he would have played a crucial role in that process. As it happened, Alexander annexed Punjab, but placed his worthy foe, Porus, back on his throne: the Greek soldiers were homesick and wanted to return to their Mediterranean homeland'.

Sujata stopped for a moment. Perhaps her discourse on history was falling on deaf ears, she feared. But she was relieved to see the Greek professor in the front row leaning forward attentively. Still, perhaps it was time, she thought, to bring in the management discipline into the 'show'.

'We can say without hesitation that the roots of the management discipline go back to the time of Alexander. He exhibited great leadership qualities, refusing to drink water when his soldiers lacked water, and always leading by example. In those irresistible and decisive flank attacks by the Greek army, when a smaller group broke off and rode down the sides of the enemy army to attack its flanks, it was always Alexander who led the charge'.

Sujata paused again and then smiled broadly at the delegates. 'I would also like to point out that Kerala has a long seacoast, with warm tropical waters. I know that the Greeks are lovers of the sea. I remember hearing about a bunch of Greek soldiers who had lost their bearings after a battle and were wandering around. After moving in different directions, they suddenly came upon the sea. Overwhelmed with joy, they shouted excitedly, 'thalassa, thalassa', the Greek word for sea, I believe'. As the Greek delegates broke out into prolonged laughter, she added: 'so you see, Kerala is an ideal place for you as a conference destination!'

'Her speech gave the conference a great launching pad', Rakesh told Divya.  "The Canadian professor, his name is Morrison, if I'm not mistaken, who is here to sign the faculty exchange agreement with IIMK, rose and shook her hand enthusiastically when she sat down after the speech. He loved it'.

Morrison in from McGill, isn't he?', Divya asked.

'No, from the University of Western Ontario in London - Canada', it was Roshan who answered.

'I believe the faculty exchange programme will take off next term itself. The details are yet to be worked out, about the length of the stay, financing from both sides and all that. But Jose told me that Dr. Sujata and Morrison have struck it off very well, that the deliberations have been fruitful'.

'But, Roshan, tell Divya also about the fiasco parts of the conference, the real juicy stuff'.

'You are right; she'll get a kick out of that. You know, Divya, one conference presentation was so awful that Dr. Morrison, who was beaming after then inaugural session, left the room in disgust'.

'I'm all ears', Divya said, excited about the promised juicy stuff.

In fact, Roshan had heard about the awful session from

Sujata herself. Sujata was also clear in her mind about the large incidence of bad papers accepted for the conference. After the first day's presentations she had called an emergency meeting of the conference committee and gave the members a piece of her mind:

'I think you people made a fundamental mistake in assessing papers based on the abstracts submitted. I really can't see why you took such an ill-advised decision. It seems like you came to the consensus, "if the author is from a recognized institution in India, let's accept his abstract". And, look at the result: a group walk-out from a presentation'.

Sujata was referring to the presentation by a young assistant professor from a new institution in Kerala itself. He had been a successful small-scale businessman, who had for some reason turned to academics–but without taking a research degree. He may have wanted to make a mark even by shocking his audience so that they would remember him and his contribution. He had started in a dull fashion, talking vaguely about the philosophy of management, and the audience had lapsed into a pleasant low-buzz of conversation among themselves. Then, all of a sudden, the delegate turned to the whiteboard and dashed across it in bold letters the most famous and path-breaking equation of all time:

$$E = mc^2$$

It was not apparent to anyone in the puzzled audience why he had written the equation, for he had not been talking of Einstein or about any subject related to physics. Then the man continued talking about the philosophy of management –which, to do him justice, he had alluded to in his abstract–and, then, as suddenly as before, turned to the whiteboard and wrote:

FUCk  You.        OK !

Having done his handicraft, he turned around and stood grinning as if asking, 'wasn't that a stroke of genius on my part?'

The response was immediate. Barring a few who were sleeping or sleepy enough not to comprehend what was happening, the audience left the room. Dr. Morrison was gracious enough to pretend that he had received an urgent message, looking intently at his mobile as he left the room.

But the IIMK students who were present in the hall were not prepared to take such nonsense without striking back. It was not clear which student did it, for a group of them had walked to the exit circling the delegate. The delegate noticed some of the sarcastic smiles of those looking at the board while leaving.  So he turned around to look too. It was written therein outsized letters:

$$U = I^2$$

where  U = you;  I = idiot

He turned around to face the decimated audience again with a sheepish smile but made his business short. He made a few vague statements and then wound up saying, 'thank you, that was all', then leaving the hall and the campus never to be seen again, not even at the final day's cultural extravaganza at Taj hotel.

'Mind you, this was not the only fiasco among the presentations', Sujata told the conference committee members shifting uneasily in their chairs. I am not denying there were good papers presented; most of the ones from

IIMK and the Greek delegates held a high standard, and the delegates were able to hold the attention of the audience and generate fruitful discussions. But Dr. Morrison came to me genuinely puzzled after a talk by a delegate from Bangalore University, and asked: "Dr. Sujata, what was he talking about? Rather, I should ask what was he not talking about - for it seems to me that he touched upon all possible topics: the history of the homo sapiens, that of India, the stock market, environmental degradation, agricultural reforms, the list runs on. I must say I wondered how such a paper could have been accepted for the conference".

I was red-faced, I imagine, filled with shame to have had to hear this from the head of an institution that is going to collaborate with us on research and teaching. Now, I wonder too, like Dr. Morrison, how this paper's abstract could have been considered acceptable; or was it so that any paper from Bangalore, The Silicon Valley of India is automatically accepted for our conferences?'

'How awful! Divya exclaimed after Roshan had narrated the incident. 'I feel sorry for Dr. Sujata. How could such clowns enter our famed institution in the garb of competent researchers? I must say that I think the conference committee slipped up badly. Dr. Sujata couldn't have been expected to sit and go through abstracts'.

'Naa....I think the man just made a wrong judgment'. Roshan played the incident down–perhaps because he was in the team that judged abstracts. 'I think he thought he could distinguish himself in this crazy manner, that's all. And don't lose sight of the fact that some very good papers were presented as the director herself pointed out'.

He turned to Rakesh. 'Am I right, Dr. Rakesh? I overheard Dr. Morrison telling the director that some of the papers presented should be channeled into well-known international scholarly journals'.

'I suppose he meant that just bringing out conference proceedings is not sufficient', Rakesh responded. 'If some papers get published in well-known journals, IIMK can bring out reprints of those, make that a regular series'.

Rakesh got up from the awkward leaning position he had been holding in the rapid, smooth movement'. Like a cat, Divya thought.

'Let's not waste more time discussing paper presentations', he made a dismissing motion with his hand. "Now about tomorrow: are all arrangements in place for the evening? I just hope that creep, Mohan, is not going to put a damper on the proceedings. I don't know if you guys know this, but he is the auditor for this programme. He has managed to do something crude already, charging a Greek delegate for bringing his wife along'.

'What, for bringing his wife?', Divya asked incredulously.

'Yes, because she will be with him for the cultural programme and dinner tomorrow. Mohan insists that the conference fee does not include dinner for spouses!'

'Fantastic hospitality by IIMK! '

'I could take this up with the director, but the damage has been done already as the Greek delegate has been informed and charged. But what you could do, Divya is to talk with the Greek gentleman tomorrow and explain that it was all a mistake. A woman's touch is needed after the gross intervention by our master schemer'.

'Sure. And shall I also tell him that the money will be refunded? I am sure that we can raise the amount between us'.

'You took the words out of my mouth', Rakesh said in admiration. This girl is so quick off the mark, he told himself.


Roshan and Divya had seen to it that things were indeed in place for the cultural extravaganza on the final evening of the conference. Two rooms had been booked at the Taj hotel for Shalini   and her students – and their mothers - as there was no green room attached to the performance hall. The Vasco de Gama was to be the venue of the dance performances but to be kept alcohol-free unlike during the IIMk student parties. There would indeed be cocktails for the delegates, but they were to be served in the hall upstairs where Divya had once come across Rakesh and his boy-friend–in what she was still reluctant to call a compromising situation. The dinner would be then served in the banquet hall where Divya had made the acquaintance of the Filipino singer of the touring band.

The evening programme went like clockwork. To start with, the delegates were given a taste of Kerala's martial art, 'Kalari Payattu'. The show was held on the expansive hall outside the Gama Hall, the spectators standing around the lawn in small groups, or alone, watching the agile, acrobatic movements: observing silently, but gasping occasionally as the performers leaped high into the air as they swung short swords and shields.

Sujata and Dr. Morrison stood together in one corner of the lawn. At one stage when she looked at the visitor to see how he liked the show, she was shocked–for he had a troubled look on his frank countenance. Concerned, she asked, raising her voice above the sound of the clash of metal upon metal,

'Why, what is the matter, Dr. Morrison, are you unwell?'

'Oh no', Morrison shook himself out of a kind of stupor he seemed to have been in. 'Great show, I am thoroughly enjoying it. Remarkable skills. So young too, the performers'.

But Sujata was not to be deflected that easily. If the distinguished visitor had a serious problem, it was her duty to find out about it and possibly solve the issue.

'True. But I can see that you are worried about something. Seriously worried, I might say. Please do feel free to open up to me. What am I here for otherwise as your host?'

Morrison moved unobtrusively away from a group of delegates he had been standing adjacent to.

'All right, Sujata, you are a keen observer. Something is troubling me. But this is no place to discuss it. Also, why spoil a wonderful evening? Could I talk to you tomorrow about this?'

'Certainly. We could do one thing. The other delegates are all headed for the Wayanad mountain region tomorrow on a trekking trip. We could, instead, have our discussion on this sensitive topic tomorrow, but not on campus, on a trip of our own. Why not to a historical site: the beach where Vasco de Gama landed in 1498, the first European visit after Alexander, ushering in the colonial age in India?'

'That would be better. Let's keep this lovely evening problem-free!'

'But, then, promise to put it out of your mind now. See there, those girls are using the weapon called the 'urumi': a deadly, long, flexible double-edged blade that can be rolled up and kept in your waist. They are swinging it like a long belt'.

They stood silently, hearing the swish of the blades, a sharp hissing sound as the long blade flew through the air, unfolding and twirling.

'You said a belt. More like a whip, I think', Morrison remarked.

When the clash of metal died down, they moved to the Gama hall. Sujata had consented to the cocktails being served in the hall before the dance performance. 'But make sure that the drinks trays are cleared by the time the dancer's troop go in', she gave stern instructions to Rakesh. Good in a way, perhaps we will save half an hour, skipping the sojourn at the hall on the upper floor'.

She looked Rakesh over critically and didn't seem happy about his loose pyjama-kurta outfit. 'The intellectual look, eh? That's ok, but have you got everything in order? This is more complicated than your wild faculty-student parties. And make sure you capture the dances on video. Haven't you done it for the martial art show?'

Rakesh assured her that he had, patting his video case slung over his shoulder to show that everything is in place.

Shalini had included several dance items for the evening, taking care to keep each one fairly short - as she guessed that the attention span of the delegates, with or without cocktails, will be fairly short too. The students, only two boys included among the overwhelming majority of girls, had been divided into three groups so that as soon as one item was completed, the next one could begin, be it a solo or a group performance.

The bright dance costumes worn by the bright-faced eager young dancers caught the eyes of the delegates who became bright-eyed themselves. For one of the items, the girls came decked out in red saris. Seeing them, Morrison leaned towards Sujata and whispered, ' I didn't know your saris came in such small sizes'.

Sujata smiled and answered, again in a whisper as the musicians sitting on one side of the stage were working up a repeated beat, 'indeed, they come in all sizes, just like dancers'–even though she had a feeling that those small saris were costume-made.

Morrison mused again, loudly, 'I wonder too how these children develop such flexible bodies, bending over backwards fully, stretching out their legs fully'.

'I guess it's easy when you start young', Sujata told him. 'That's the way to do it - though you see even married women take up classical dancing in their thirties'.

Towards the end of the dance programme, Divya made a trip up to the rooms reserved for Shalini's group to check if everything was hunky-dory with them. As she got off the elevator and turned into the corridor leading to their rooms, she saw a woman running along the corridor towards her, gesticulating wildly and shouting something that she couldn't catch. As the woman came nearer, Divya could hear her more clearly.

'Catch him, he has taken nude photos and videos of our children!'.

'When, where? Where has he gone?', Divya shouted back.

But she at once realized that she had herself seen a man hurrying away at the far end of the corridor, opening a service door exit and going through that. They would never be able to catch him now.

'Did you get a good look at him?', she asked as she held the woman and tried to console her.

'No, I was in the adjacent room, dressing up my daughter'. The words came out slowly, intermittently, between bouts of sobbing. 'I heard a man's voice and went over to see what was happening. It took some time as I hadn't quite finished with my daughter. When I reached the room, I found a man taking videos of the children moving around naked as they searched for and changed dresses. He sensed my presence behind him, I think. He turned around covering his face and quickly pushed past me, roughly shouldering me aside. I can only say that he looked fit, fairly young'.

Divya talked gently with the children who didn't seem to be aware of the gravity of the violation of the crime committed. 'That uncle', said one small girl, screwing up her eyes, 'said he is taking photos to make new dance dresses for us. But, shame-shame no, I held a pillow in front of me'.

There was only one dance remaining in the performance calendar for the evening and that went off without a hitch, met by rounds of applause. The children had not been disturbed by the incident that had their mothers in hysterics. It took a lot of effort by the IIMK conference organizers to calm these ladies down, and it was finally Shalini who managed that, promising them that the evil intruder will be caught and punished.

Shalini had opted for the Taj buffet for her troupe, and the kids trooped off happily to the long buffet table, unaware of the crisis that their parents were passing through. Divya and Roshan ushered the delegates to the regular dining hall, where to Divya's surprise and joy, the Filipino band still held the fort. The band was playing, but on seeing Divya, Rachel left the stage with a quick excuse conveyed to the drummer and ran over to the new arrivals. She reached Divya's side just when the IIMK group was dispersing across several tables. Divya was already seated next to Dr. Morrison, and Dr. Rubin, the other foreigner who was not part of the delegates, was standing beside them exchanging a few words before moving on to the seat Sekhar had kept for him.

Divya introduced the Filipino girl to both Morrison and Rubin. Morrison smiled broadly, saying that he had several Filipino friends in Canada. 'Actually, my wife', he corrected. 'She seems to have something in common with you Filipino girls', he said, to Divya's glad surprise with a naughty wink that was out of keeping with his solemn professional bearing.

'We Filipinos have something of everyone in us', Rachel responded and both she and Morrison burst into laughter. Then Rachel turned to Rubin and asked,' and how about you, have you come across me singing in a band in any of your cruises around the world?' Rubin smiled too, a smile that did not reach his eyes, Divya thought. 'Sorry, never had the pleasure', he said rather curtly, and then, inclining his head at Morrison, walked over to join Sekhar.

Rachel pulled Divya up from her seat, saying, 'excuse me, Mr. Morrison, I have a few complaints about this young lady'. She pulled Rachel away from the table and into the small corridor that leads to the dressing rooms–and then swerves away to the lobby–from the dining room.

'So, you stayed longer than originally planned', Divya remarked happily. 'We ought to meet regularly, at least a few times before you finally leave'.

'Oh, not to worry, there is plenty of time Divya. We will be here for another four months till the spring season starts in Europe', Rachel gave the thumbs-up sign. 'But tell me Divya, who is that creep? He gives me the creeps'.

'You mean....'

'No, not the jovial Canadian. I could take him to be my doting uncle. The other man. Something indescribably nasty about him, I feel it in my bones. You know, I have always had these intuitive feelings and premonitions, and my friends and family say these turn out to be true always'.

'He works with that young professor, Sekhar, whom he joined for dinner just now. Just a visiting researcher: one hardly notices him, he keeps aloof too'.

'Well, you'd better notice him, keep an eye on him. I tell you, he is upto no good'.

Divya was about to reply but was startled to feel a hand on her shoulder. Sujata had come from the lobby through the small winding corridor and had paused beside the two friends. 'Oh no, she is sure to have overheard us, bad talk about faculty and all that', Divya cursed herself for not keeping an eye out for roaming IIMK folk. But she said,' oh, hello madam, we didn't see you', and introduced Rachel to her.

Sujata looked over Rachel unapologetically almost from toe to head, making no effort to hide her interest. Rachel watched her with a smile on her face but did not make any bold – and perhaps provocative - remark that Divya was afraid she might come up with.

'Yes, Divya has told me about you', Sujata now smiled warmly at the Filipino girl. 'Really nice to have met you finally; come over to our institute one day as my personal guest'.

Rachel too had been looking over Sujata, but covertly, and seemed to have liked what she observed. She warmly responded to Sujata's invitation.

'I will, Professor, I would be glad to. But let me now leave you together. You must have so much to discuss and plan, with so many guests to take care of for the rest of the evening'.

'Yes, but make sure they play the music for your favourite song', Sujata called out as the young Filipino ran briskly back to her band through the corridor'.

'I'm sorry, Dr. Sujata…….', Divya stammered.

Sujata held up her hand as if to silence her. 'Yes, I did hear what Rachel said', she said thoughtfully. 'Normally I would take it to be the ramblings, figments of the imagination of an immature mind, but….', she halted mid-way into the sentence.

'Yes, Dr. Sujata?'

'Your Rachel seems to be very sound of body and mind. So, I wouldn't dismiss her intuition as rubbish'.

Then she walked down the narrow corridor towards the table where Dr. Morrison was sitting, not even sparing a sideways glance at the nearby table occupied by the other visitor to the institute.

# XVIII

'I won't push it. Let him open up when he feels inclined to', Sujata told herself. She and Morrison had left the IIMK campus later than planned, reaching the Kappad beach only by ten o'clock. Fortunately, it being winter–if you can call 24 degrees C winter temperature–in Kerala, the sun was still benign at that time of the day. They had exchanged only a few words on the way to the historical site, both using the car ride to send off pending email messages.

Even when they walked on the lonely beach, with only seabirds waiting patiently to catch prey washed in by the waves for company, Morrison seemed reluctant to discuss what he evidently considered a very sensitive matter. Sujata, throwing a glance at him, was not surprised, for the man's ruddy frank face and steady eyes sent a message of trustworthiness and adherence to commitments.

'So, this is where the blighter landed', Morrison said jovially, but it was clear that it was not a sarcastic remark about a great explorer who opened up a new world–for Europeans.

'Yes, possibly on the rocky part where a lighthouse has stood for centuries', Sujata pointed to a structure whose outlines were not very clear from where they stood. 'But I must say that an alternate hypothesis suggests a spot further along the coast'.

'But I see no monuments'.

'There is one, but hardly noticeable. Fishermen's families use it to dry clothes!'

'So, the spice trade that brought wealth to the coast also brought colonizers. You know, Dr.Sujata, once I read an article by a Canadian sociologist about how such a turn of events might have thwarted a native industrial revolution in Kerala'.

'How interesting! I have not seen that article. What is the name of that Canadian sociologist?'

'I don't remember. Too bad, but that it the way it is! I have a great memory for faces, facts, and data, but not for names. I just remember that it was a female sociologist working at a Canadian university'.

'And, so, what was her thesis about Kerala?'

'Well, what she argued was that in the fifteenth century, conditions were ideal for a native industrial revolution in Kerala. There was technical innovation, even if on a small scale, and liquidity and wealth from trade. Also, as importantly, the structure of the Kerala society with its independent chieftains was more similar to feudal Japan and Europe, rather than to the large river valley empires. She reasoned that the arrival of the Europeans, together with a blockade of sea-trading routes by non-European powers, prevented an incipient industrial revolution in Kerala'.

'Trade has always been the lifeline of a nation', Sujata agreed, 'so a blockade of trading routes would have throttled that flowering industrialization. It seems that the current debate on the relative merits of trade-oriented and closed economies has to be extended back to those pre-colonial times'.

'Further back, Dr. Sujata, further back, just as you hinted at in your inaugural address. Leadership, brand image, all buzz words in management today were key factors even in ancient times. Phoenicians, the ancient trading community who are said to have brought literacy to the Greeks, had a branded product: the purple-dyed cloth that was famed all across the global trading nations'.

They walked in silence along the seafront for a few minutes. 'I hope he is now in a state of mind, de-stressed and relaxed on this isolated beach, to begin talking on that sensitive issue, whatever it may be', Sujata thought. But then perhaps his mind has to be taken back to the previous evening, which was when he first aired his misgivings, though very vaguely.

'So, how did you enjoy the performance by students last evening?'

'Wonderful, really wonderful', Morrison beamed. 'This was the first time I watched an Indian cultural performance, since seeing one on Canadian TV some years ago'.

'On TV? A soap opera, I would guess'.

'Not really', Morrison laughed. 'Actually, my wife used to watch it and I sat with her only during a few episodes'.

'What was it about? Indian dances again?'

'Oh no. Something totally different, rather intriguing. It was about an Indian woman who sings hymns to an Indian god, who suddenly starts appearing in an empty TV channel for her'.

'Lucky woman! Her wish was granted, eh?'

'You could say that. But perhaps she got more than what she bargained for. For, after a few gracious appearances, the god makes amorous suggestions to her'.

'What! Does she then enter the TV or does he hop out?'

'I can't tell you because I stopped watching it. I don't even remember the name of that Canadian TV serial. I told you I have a poor memory for names, didn't I? However, I could ask my wife when I am back home and tell you if you would like to know'.

'You should have kept an eye on your wife, Dr. Morrison', Sujata said, adopting a serious, worried tone. 'Are you sure that God did not materialize in an empty channel for her too?'

'You are right', Morrison guffawed. 'I ought to have been more alert to the fallouts of such a show!'.

Suddenly, with no prologue, but as Sujata had expected, he started talking about what had been troubling him since the conference began.

'You are right, Dr. Sujata, something has been on my mind since the very first session of the conference. I didn't want to jump to any unfounded conclusions; that's why I didn't broach the matter thus far. But now I feel you should know about it, even before I have all facts in black and white'.

Sujata didn't interrupt, stood listening, eyes on the far horizon.

'You'll be shocked, I dare say. It concerns Rubin, your

visiting research fellow. He is not what he seems to be, what he makes out himself to be. I believe he has a criminal record'.

Sujata was taken aback but did not interrupt.

'That first session when he came in, his face rang a bell for me. I knew I had seen him earlier, and then in some unpleasant circumstances. I believe he is wanted by the Canadian Police for involvement in some illegal activity, possibly of a gross nature. It was a university that sounded the alarm, I think'.

Now Sujata could not help interrupting, unable to hold back her anxiety.

'Rubin a criminal? I am shocked! What kind?'

'I am unable to supply that information to you now. I cannot recollect what that look-out notice given out by the authorities back home had to do with'.

Perhaps he does have an inkling, Sujata told herself. He must be playing safe - in case it turns out on further investigations that he has goofed up.

'I suppose he came with good references', Morrison looked at her questioningly. 'But that's not difficult because the referees are usually not aware of the non-academic lives of the person under review: they are only looking at academic achievements and promise'.

'Yes, he had good references. Sekhar did check all that, I believe. It is the department's responsibility to do that before the name is passed on to me for approval. He has an EU passport; not sure what nationality he possessed originally'.

'Your description fits the person I am referring to–I

mean, the one who I think is the same as your visitor'.

'So what do you suggest I do now? Should I inform the police, rather than the foreign ministry, get him apprehended?'

'No, no, that would be too premature. As I see it, there is no hurry, he–if he is indeed the one I suspect him to be– is comfortable, feeling secure, perhaps also feeling free to pursue his anti-social activities. You could keep an eye on him, wait till you hear from me. I'll check with Canadian authorities and get back to you soon after I return home. There will not be any delay; I should be in touch with you with definite information within a week after I get back'.

'Fair enough. He has the whole of two terms here, has signed up to give lectures too, so shouldn't be traveling except to nearby tourist spots. I'll plan to observe him at those locations'.

'I have to apologize, Dr. Sujata, for having taken up so much time, brought you to this beach away from your responsibilities, to discuss this miscreant. We should have been discussing the exchange programme today, according to our drawn-up schedules'

'Well, this is important too, terribly important. And we have had an excellent beginning in making preliminary plans for the exchange programme. Everything is right on track, as I see it'.

Morrison smiled, almost gratefully, Sujata thought, and she smiled right back. By mutual consent they headed back towards the car bearing the sign, 'Government of India', a sign which almost works like an ambulance siren in getting the vehicle and its occupants through traffic blocks and even violent demonstrations. They walked along the edge of the waterfront, the waves breaking long before the shoreline and coming in at knee-height.

Suddenly Morrison halted abruptly. Sujata looked at him, a little concerned. Had he remembered something that he ought to have said - was it more bad news, perhaps about mafia backing that strengthens the hand of the man under suspicion?

But Morrison had come to an abrupt standstill only to avoid crunching under his feet a crab scuttling away from a marauding seabird.

# XIX

The very next weekend - after the echoes of the conference had died down - Divya was at Shalini's door early in the forenoon. She was bubbling with enthusiasm and wanted to convey all the praise that had been showered on Shalini's student brigade by the delegates from India and abroad alike.

As Divya turned into the gateway, she paused and looked at the adjoining house grounds. No sign of the housekeeper. A couple of times more Divya had observed her in intimate conversation with the meddlesome–and vaguely forbidding - food delivery man. On those occasions, the woman had ignored Divya's presence. However, once when Divya saw her alone, clearing fallen leaves, she had waved a short greeting. Now there was no sign of her.

As Divya reached the porch, a cat raised itself lazily from the doormat, stretching elaborately. Then it walked away slowly in a dignified manner, not deigning to look at Divya. This happened every time she went there, but the cats and the doormats changed colour frequently. Perhaps, it is just the same cat all the time, Divya smiled at the stray, fuzzy thought: a chameleon-cat!

Divya kept her shoes outside and pushed the front door open. The sound of music and the patter of dancing feet could be heard from the large room inside with a square at the centre. Shalini was wasting no time, was back to her regular schedule that had been interrupted by the IIMK global conference. Often she stood in front of the dancing students, beating the rhythm with a wooden rod, but now she was dancing, demonstrating steps to the students.

Not wishing to interrupt the session, Divya backed off from the door of the dance hall. The classes would go on for an hour or so. She was undecided about whether to stay or return later in the evening. Then she had an idea: might as well water the plants in the garden, then she can decide whether to stay or leave.

Contrary to her usual routine, this time she started by watering the plants by the boundary wall against the house rented by the mysterious IIM professor. The bougainvilleas stood swaying their red, yellow, and light-pink flowers in the gentle breeze as she attended to them. Then, suddenly, she was startled by the popping up of a head from the other side of the wall as if it had been lying in wait for her. It was the housekeeper.

To Divya's surprise, the woman could speak English and was aware of the fact that Divya was not from Kerala.

'I see you always in the garden, nice to finally meet you', the woman gushed. 'Sir' has said that you are also from IIM. She had a honey-coloured face, with thick eyebrows and small, shrewd, shifty eyes. Divya had thought at first sight that she was of slight build, but could now notice her powerful, gnarled arms that spoke of a life spent in hard toil.

, By 'sir' she obviously meant the master of the house, Divya guessed.

'And, what is the name of sir?'

'I just call him sir', was the curt, evasive answer that clearly brooked no further enquiry on the matter.

The woman said that she had been working in Dubai for many years with a North Indian family and could speak Hindi well too. She hailed from the south of Kerala but had no family left there.

After some commonplace talk, the woman turned to take a long look at the house and said in a low voice:

'The pay is extremely good, and the work is light, but I will not stay long'.

'And why would that be?', Divya tried to sound casual and uninterested.

'Sir is good. He even has many paintings in the hall upstairs. Many of them he has done himself. He is popular too. Many friends come to the house, foreigners, and children too'.

'Well, that's nice!'

'Yes, maybe. But he has other pictures and films as well. I saw him and his friend watching them in a room upstairs. Chi, chi, chi, very bad, not nice at all. Chi chi chi'. She shook her head vehemently.

Divya did not interrupt, though her heartbeat had quickened in anticipation.

'Very bad. Vulgar. Chi chi. Films of children without clothes, together with men. I had a good look when sir was watching with a friend'.

'Oh, that is very bad indeed', Divya shouted in anger, aid, blood rushing to her face.

The woman put a finger to her lips, indicating Divya should keep her voice down.

'I understand now why you want to leave. But the police should be informed about this'.

A cunning look flitted across the woman's face. 'Sir has a friend from IIM also who comes here. He was there with sir'.

'Where? '

'In that room with sir, looking at the dirty pictures of children'.

There was a tight feeling in Divya's chest. 'You know his name?'

'Sir told me, but I have forgotten'. She seemed genuinely angry with herself for forgetting the name, hitting her head with her palm.

'Too bad, 'sir' had asked me to tell you '.Having blurted out the truth by mistake, she hastily corrected herself: 'I mean sir asked me not to tell you. You see', the cunning look again crossed her face, 'sir has seen you in the garden and knows you from IIM'.

After having dealt these multiple blows to Divya, the woman excused herself saying she had some work inside, and retreated quickly into the house.

Divya was in a totally confused state of mind. She felt an intuitive dislike for that woman–and distrusted her words. Yet, she had a feeling that there was a grain of truth in what she said and felt helpless, unable to separate the wheat from the chaff.

She continued to water the plants mechanically. Perhaps I should go back now, she thought, put off talking to Shalini about the conference accolades for her and her students to another visit. She somehow didn't relish the thought of meeting Shalini right then after hearing about the evil that had afflicted that neighbourhood, in the form of a virtual Satan from her institution.

BY then she had reached the backside wall, moving from plant to plant. It was then that the nightingale broke out into its long, repeated calls that merged into a melodious song. Even in her bewildered state of mind, Divya strained her neck trying to get a look at it. Remembering what Shalini had told her, she moved to the corner of the backside wall that reached behind the neighbouring house, to see the singing nightingale.

Yes, there it was, just as Shalini had said, partly hidden among the mango leaves. Divya watched it, standing still, for a long while. Then, against her will, and the diktat imposed by Shalini, her eyes turned to the backside windows of the adjoining house.

A man was standing with his back to the window, talking to someone inside the room. Then, as Divya watched, he turned around to face the window.

Divya stood transfixed with horror.

It was Rakesh.

She would recognize his clear-cut profile in a sea of faces, let alone at a window lit up by the morning sun.

True to his word, Morrison did not delay in getting in touch with Sujata after his return to The University of Western Ontario. His confidential note sent through Fed Express delivery was brief and to the point.

Dear Dr. Sujata,

He is what I thought he was.

A criminal of the worst kind: a paedophile, he is active in producing and circulating child pornography, driven by commercial interest and his perversion.

But now his cool sojourn at your institute will be soon over. The Canadian authorities are contacting their Indian counterparts; the net is closing around him.

You don't have to initiate any action, just keep him under surveillance.

Morrison

Sujata showed Jose–whom she had taken into confidence regarding Morrison's revelation on the beach–

the letter.

'We will keep him under observation', Jose said, trying to sound calm, but Sujata could see that he was shaken badly by the immensity of the misfortune that had befallen IIMK in the shape of Rubin, an academic visitor invited over like so many others.

'He has lectures scheduled well into the next month', Jose added. 'So, he is unlikely to undertake any sightseeing trips, other than short day trips. Anyhow, housekeeping will know if he starts packing'.

'Good. That's all we need to do, keep an eye on him', Sujata nodded. 'And, pray that we will never see his kind again at this institute or in our lives ever again'.

# XXI

It was the big-built girl occupying the room next to Divya who saved her life. An unlikely savior, since the two girls hardly ever saw each other. Divya spent most of her time doing her assignments in an isolated corner of the sprawling library, while the girl next door was always away working jointly in a study group.

'I was passing by the door', the girls told Sujata, emphasizing her words with dramatic gestures, 'when I heard this horrid, sorry, terrible gasping sound. Divya's door was open, probably because she had latched it wrongly in a hurry. I hesitated a moment, but then pushed the door open. She was lying stretched out on the floor, arms flung out. There was foam at her mouth and she had vomited all over the place'.

Though it had been a close brush with death by self-inflicted poisoning, Divya was very quickly beyond danger, treated at the Nirmala Hospital. In fact, the chief physician there said that she could be taken back after a day to the infirmary on the IIMK campus, run by the same hospital.

'I have failed Divya's parents miserably, the thought kept coming back to haunt Sujata. But, the woman of action that she was she always dismissed the thought at once: what was important now was to find the reason for the girl's tragic act and to punish the ones who had brought her to that state. It was also clear to Sujata that it would be best for the girl to drop out of the course temporarily. She could return the next year for the program and be given credits for the part of the program already completed before tragedy struck. It would be too dangerous, too imprudent, to let her remain after recovering physically. Certain people and events had come together in some unexplained pattern to pose a life-threatening danger to Divya. Even if these people and events were identified – as Sujata intended to, and promised herself she would–it would take time for the air to clear, to be certain that there were no lingering aftereffects or side-effects of the reign of those dangerous forces.

Sujata allowed no one access to Divya. She would be flown out with a couple of trusted secretaries when she recovered sufficiently enough to undertake travel. It would be too dangerous to allow anyone on campus to meet her when it was unclear what caused the girl to go over the edge. What was puzzling to Sujata was that the girl had chosen not to confide in anyone: not in Roshan, Rakesh, or Sujata herself - to whom Divya has a special kind of access not open to other students.

She met Divya only once after the girl was brought back to the campus infirmary. Divya was lying with her eyes open, gazing at the ceiling, a vacant, blank look on her face. The girl tried valiantly to sit up straight on the bed when Sujata entered the room and even said a few lines:

'I am sorry, Dr. Sujata….'

Sujata said nothing at first, but sitting on the bed, held the girl's hands together in her own for a long while, and then stroked the pallid cheeks.

'It was not your fault, Divya, don't take the blame upon yourself, it was we, the institute, who failed you'.

Tears filled the girl's eyes. Sujata stroked them away gently with her hand.

'But soon you will be home with your parents. You can come back to the MBA program next year. And, don't bother to give any explanations now. I will find out who caused you such anguish and deal with them. I can promise you that'.

Divya tried to say something, but Sujata stroked her cheeks again, indicating to her to stay silent and conserve her energy.

'And when you come back to rejoin, it will just as when you came last year, with dreams and hopes. Unlimited possibilities will again open up for you, Divya. This green campus will be waiting for you with all those possibilities'.

As she sat at her table, ostensibly immersed in a research report, Sujata's logical mind was racing through the possible reasons for the disaster that had struck Divya and the institute, rejecting some outright, marking down others mentally as worthy of investigation. The rigorous IIMK academic schedule could hardly be a reason, she figured. Divya had been doing very well, and there had been no feedback from teachers or program secretaries about any stressed reaction or outburst on her part. In fact, in the light of Divya's parents' request for special consideration for the girl, Sujata had put in place a non-intrusive observation of the girl by her trusted lieutenants, and they had reported nothing abnormal, at least not in the academic sphere.

So, the igniting spark of the calamity had not come from the formal academic program, Sujata concluded. Failed romance, as earlier in her life? Threats of retaliation from a group that had spread its influence to the institute, from a shadowy drug fraternity?

Her thoughts were interrupted by Bhaskaran poking his head into the room, his large body hidden well behind the door.

'Madam, systems manager Mohan and faculty member Sekhar are here to see you. They have no appointment but say it is very important, something about Diya.

Sujata looked at her watch. 'But I had called the student Elizabeth over, is she delayed?'

'No madam, she is here, but says she does not mind waiting, that the faculty members can meet you first'.

They always appear together, Sujata thought as the two staff members trooped in. But, of these days, if the one coming to ask for a raise is accompanied by the other for moral support, I will kick the supporter out.

They look happy and confident, it struck Sujata. Odd - given the circumstances prevailing at the institute.

'Well, what is it?', she raised her voice. 'This is no time for petty campus complaints, after such a tragedy involving one of our students'.

'We understand, madam', Mohan said, trying unsuccessfully to sound obsequious—he was in a jubilant mood always when then institute suffered a setback as this seemed to increase the importance of the system manager's role.

'This is no ordinary campus matter we have come to raise with you. It is about Divya'.

'What about her, the poor girl? Are you saying that you know the reason for her extreme step?'

'Could be so, madam, that's what we came to keep you posted. But we have two alternate explanations;

Sujata sat back straight in her chair, genuinely interested now.

'The first explanation has to do with Dr. Rakesh', Sekhar said, expecting to see his director's shapely jaw drop in astonishment. But Sujata sat still, seemingly unmoved.

'You see, madam, Divya came to know from Roshan that Rakesh is "gay". That would have come as a great shock to her. And we have to keep in mind that it was common knowledge that she had a crush on him. I noticed myself the effect on her in an indirect way: her marks in my course dipped after Rakesh 'came out of the closet', or, rather, was identified for what he is'.

'But her final grade for your course was good, wasn't it so?'

'True, that's right, madam', Sekhar said hastily. But we are informed that Divya has peaks and troughs when under stress. So, a peak could be followed by a bout of depression. A peak would have been the state when she thought her emotions for Rakesh were or could be, reciprocated'.

'I see, so you figure that in a severe attack of depression after the revelation about Rakesh, she tried to take her own life. And what is the other hypothesis?'

'As always, madam, as we warned you earlier about, the shadowy ways of the drug mafia', Sekhar said eagerly. 'We believe that Divya had come upon some student links with drug suppliers. She would have been then subject to threats of retaliation from these groups if she meant to disclose these links'.

'In fact', Mohan broke in to point out, 'Roshan told us that once a car tried to run her down. So, the threat was very real, not imaginary'.

'I too have heard about that incident', Sujata said thoughtfully. 'I see what you are getting at. With that threat hovering over her, she would have been unable to communicate her observations to anyone; so, the pressure would have built upon her to breaking point'.

'Precisely, madam', Sekhar said, almost triumphantly, moving forward to the edge of his seat, 'In fact, we believe this second alternative to be the more plausible explanation.'

'Yes, madam, that is our judgment', Mohan said with a satisfied look.

Sujata regarded the pair in front of her in silence for a few moments, drumming her fingers on the table, making the duo rather uncomfortable.

'Your points are well taken', she said finally. 'But we need more to go on. I suggest that you talk to more people, staff, faculty, and students, even housekeeping, and report back to me next week with your additional findings. We can then match them—I mean your findings—with the information I will receive from other sources'.

She could see that her hint about an independent investigation on her own had made the two nosey staff members rather uneasy. But they left saying, 'thank you Dr. Sujata', still upbeat, making an undertaking to return next week with more evidence to back their claims.

Sujata had the student Elizabeth called in at once. The girl sat before her uncertainly, the disarming smile Sujata remembered seeing on her face replaced by a look of profound gloom.

'I am very sorry about Divya', Sujata said softly. 'I know you are very close to her, that you have been project-mates'.

'Yes, madam', the girl said looking down. Tears dropped on to her crumpled violet blouse.

'I want you to pay attention', Sujata said, trying to revive the girl, but in a kind voice. 'I am trying to get to the bottom of this sordid, tragic affair and punish the guilty ones who brought your friend to the brink of disaster, death itself. So, I want you to help me in every way you can'.

Elizabeth wiped her tears away and sat up, with an alert look now on her face.

'Roshan told me that Divya had come upon a drug-addicted student in the hostel, a girl student, staggering around, falling. The name is Shyama. I am asking you because I am informed that you have worked together with this girl also for a term paper presentation. Do you know anything about this girl's habits, extra-curricular, and social activities?'

'Shyama, madam?', Elizabeth said, a look of incredulity on her face. 'That cannot be. Impossible, madam, Shyama is a superb athlete, very clean-living clean living. No boy on campus can pip her in a middle-distance race'.

'But Divya's observation then? Staggering, falling in

the corridor late at night?'

'Late at night? Shyama would return then after working with her study group', Elizabeth said, clearly puzzled. Then her face cleared.

'Oh, I see it now, madam. Shyama wears contact lenses of very high power–for distance vision, not for reading. She takes these off at night as her eyes get irritated with longer-time use. And, she is blind as a bat without her lenses'.

Sujata and the student looked at each other, both enlightened at the same time. And, despite the gravity of the situation, they broke out laughing.

'Blind as a bat, eh?', Sujata said to herself when Elizabeth had left. 'That certainly takes the sting out of the role of drug mafia, though, of course, it still cannot be ruled out totally'.

She rang for Bhaskaran, who materialized at once as if out of empty air.

'I'm expecting a call in exactly ten minutes. Make sure it is received on the secure line. Exactly ten minutes, get it?'

'Of course, madam. But, madam, one more person is here to see you. A student'.

'Who is it? Didn't you tell him or her I am not seeing anyone now'?

Bhaskaran scratched his head, looking embarrassed. "Yes, madam, but he said it concerns Divya. The boy is a friend of Ashok, whom you punished with a fine. I thought he might have something important for you madam'.

Sujata looked impatiently at her watch, but said, 'All right, send him in'.

The plump, over-fed looking boy who came in was in a state of suppressed excitement, quite out of keeping with the overall gloom pervading the campus.

'Pardon me for taking up your time, Dr. Sujata madam', he gushed. 'I and my friend need permission to talk to Divya'.

'Nonsense, you know no one is allowed to see her. Is this why you gatecrash in here and waste my time?'

'Madam, this is really of crucial importance, I would say even for the advancement of knowledge. We are studying afterlife and near-death phenomena and wish to interview Divya about her personal experience. Did she go through a corridor with a light at the end - and so on'.

It was a mystery why the fat boy did not go up in flames, given the intensity with which Sujata glared at him.

'Do you want to be whipped?'

'I beg your pardon madam, I don't understand', the plump boy cringed.

'Bhaskaran, where is the whip, get it at once', Sujata called out. She turned her head, looking around the room— and when she looked back at the boy, she could see only his well-stacked backside disappearing swiftly through the door.

Bhaskaran put only his head in, keeping the rest of his large body behind the door again.

'Madam, what did you say?', he asked, a puzzled look on his face, 'pin-code?'

Sujata looked down at the heap of papers before her. 'No, that is ok, Bhaskaran. I have it, 673 570 for Kunnamangalm,

Calicut'.

The call came exactly on time. Sujata sat listening for several minutes, saying nothing, not interrupting the caller even once. Only at the end of the call did she tell the caller, 'It will be next week then. I'll keep you informed. Be prepared to be here at short notice. I can get all the required clearances. But perhaps you can manage that yourself. Yes? I thought so'.

Sujata was just logging into her accounts next Monday morning when Jose burst into her room with no forewarning, past Bhaskaran who looked helplessly at her.

'He has fled, madam, the rascal', Jose shouted. Bhaskaran winced and put a finger to his lips, indicating the agitated secretary had better tune himself down.

'Calm down, Jose', Sujata said softly, and though she guessed immediately whom he was referring to, asked, 'who?'

'Rubin. It's all my fault, I take full blame'.

'No, you need not stick your neck out. I was expecting this. Short of locking him up, there was nothing we could do to keep him here'.

Jose tried to say something, swallowed, threw his hands up as if admitting defeat.

'So, how did it happen?'

'Madam, he had gone for his 2 hours lecture. There is a break after 45 minutes, and at that time many eyes would have been watching his moves. But he walked off after just 15 minutes, giving the students an assignment; just walked away clipping his pen to his pocket and picking up his notebook computer, never to be seen again on campus. Done in a very cunning manner'.

'Very cunning indeed. But, never mind. For us, it is good riddance, saves us a lot of formalities. And, he won't get far. Police forces in many countries and even Interpol are coupled into his case'.

Jose looked unhappy. 'But, madam, all the horrid things he might have done here....'.

'He will have to atone for those. There will be criminal charges for his child abuse here. And I think we will have sufficient evidence to nail him, just from this location'.

'But madam, evidence from whom, from where?', Jose looked totally at sea.

'All in good time, Jose. I am expecting information on this and other important related matters. And, rest assured, you will be there at the finishing line with me. You are part of my A-team, aren't you?'

Jose smiled as if in gratitude for the honour, but still looked unhappy.

Just then, an outcry was heard outside, from the lawns in front of the office. They could make out Mohan's raised voice, hoarse with excitement. He was I outside the room, looking over at the balcony and shouting,

'Hold him Ashok, don't let him escape this time'.

Sujata hastened on to the balcony overlooking the lawns, with steps leading down, Jose at her heels.

There, with his back to a hedge, and encircled by four students, stood the food delivery man, with a helmet and the whole works. He seemed at ease, balancing on the balls of his feet.

'We have him, madam', Mohan's voice still cracking at a high pitch, 'Salkara-Paragon delivery man, sometimes Swiggy, a fraud in and out'.

'They are interchangeable', Jose told Mohan, 'Swiggy takes orders for Salkara hotel too'.

'Fraud, fraud, he is an imposter', Mohan shouted again, hopping in his excitement. 'But this time he can't escape. Ashok, bring him here'.

Ashok, perhaps to impress his guide Sekhar and unofficial mentor Mohan, who were both on the spot, stepped up and swung his fist wildly at the stranger.

No one present knew exactly how it happened, but the next instant Ashok was all tied up in knots of hands and legs, unable to move. The stranger's hand rested lightly in control of Ashok's back.

Sujata then announced in a calm voice. 'It's all right boys: he is my man, an ace operator par excellence. You are lucky I intervened for he would have had all of you flat on the grass in no time at all'.

And then to the stranger, 'It's ok, you can let him go'.

The stranger pushed Ashok and, taking off his helmet he stepped forward, looking questioningly at Sujata. He must have been around 5-10 tall, of slim build, and, as Mohan noticed with a tremor of fear, moved with a kind of feline grace.

Then Mohan discovered something else to his horror. 'But this man has been at our lunch canteen, often sitting right next to us, isn't it Sekhar?'.

Sekhar nodded, clearly disturbed. 'Yes, but then he had no helmet, had a visitor's badge around his neck'.

'Courtesy me', Sujata said with a smile. 'But let us all go to my room. We have much to take care of'.

But Mohan stayed his ground. 'Who is he, Dr. Sujata? Which organization does he represent? I think he is up to no good, poking around even where only faculty members have the right to be'.

'As I said, he's my man, and I have given him leeway to do what he has done. And, let me add, I will never do anything that is against the interests of the Institute'.

Jose–and Bhaskaran, who stood a little away–nodded as if they fully trusted their director's word.

Jose ushered the stranger to the director's room. He lost no time making himself comfortable, sprawling loose-limbed on one of the large sofas.  Mohan, who had come into the room behind Sujata, looked askance at her: he had no intention of reporting his new findings and ideas concerning Divya's suicide attempt when that mysterious stranger was around.

'Guess what's on our systems manager's mind', Sujata remarked, turning to her 'man', careful not to call him by name. He and his colleague are stubborn about not discussing anything important when you are around. That being the case, why don't you tell me what you heard them say about Rakesh and Divya'.

Mohan gave a start, as did his partner–and sank weakly into an armchair beside the director's table, a safe distance away from the 'food delivery man'. He was too curious and apprehensive about what was to be divulged to Sujata, to leave the room in protest about the man's presence.

The stranger said lazily: 'I was sitting next to these gentlemen at the lunch canteen, dressed formally as a visitor, wearing an identification badge..'

No one present thought of asking him what the name on the badge was.

'So, what were they saying about Rakesh and Divya?', Sujata asked with a touch of impatience.

The man lifted his right forefinger, swung it in an arc to point it at Mohan.

'That man was speaking. He said: "it was stupid to think that Divya will go to pieces after hearing about Rakhesh preferring boys to girls. My, how confident were you on that?"'.

The stranger now moved his finger slowly until it pointed towards Sekhar.

'And that man replied, "Wait, we don't know for sure yet. She may still crack. The reaction may be taking time to set in"'.

Omar Khayyam wrote about the irreversibility of time: 'The moving finger writes; and, having writ, moves on'. But the ace operator's finger there was moving in an arc, retracing events that had happened in the past. Now the finger had moved to point at Mohan again.

'A fat chance, you....', Mohan swallowed the insult that had come to his tongue. 'She is going to the tie the 'rakhee' on him, making him her beloved, that is, beloved brother!'. He paused; brows wrinkled in thought. 'No, stronger medicine is needed in connection with Roshan's exposure to crack her'.

'And, then', Sujata prompted for the man had stopped his narration.

'And, then, the librarian came up to their table with the lunch tray and they started discussing mundane institute matters. Very boring, I must say'.

Mohan was watching the stranger with hatred from under hooded eyes. How did this fellow overhear us, we were talking in whispers, he wondered? Of course, the fellow must have had a listening device!

Sujata regarded the two inseparable staff members thoughtfully, a look that made them twitch in their seats. An important piece of information that she had received before joining passed through her mind again, that a homophobic group had been active at IIMK, had come up suddenly and died down as suddenly for no clear reason, just as had happened with the Klux-Klux- Klan. At the height of their strength they had gone around saying nasty things like: 'don't sit there, don't use that room, a "homo" has used it', and so on. Perhaps Mohan had been a sympathizer of the group, even if not an open, pledged member.

'Well, it seems that you people do not believe in your claims', she said now, sarcasm oozing in her tone.

'Which claim, madam', Sekhar said, feigning ignorance on any such discussion.

'Do I have to spell it out?', Sujata raised her voice, I am referring, of course, to your claim that the information on Rakesh's inclinations caused Divya anguish enough to try to commit suicide'.

'I beg your pardon, Dr. Sujata, but I think that the claim still stands. Divya may have taken it well, but that night depression could have hit her'. He leaned forward in his chair. 'Madam, we know that she had huge swings in moods'.

'And that she has already tried to take her own life once again for a failed love affair', Mohan added.

How did this fellow get that information about Divya's past? Sujata wondered. But she put the thought out of her mind: there was urgent work to be done right now.

Adopting a conciliatory tone, she said, 'I think that is a good point you made, Sekhar. Who knows, she might have reconciled herself to the shocking news about Rakesh, but then, perhaps, early that ill-fated morning, depression came in a deluge'.

Then she added decisively: 'Anyhow, today is not a good day to discuss the report that you both planned to present to me. I can see that you are not willing to discuss your findings when this gentleman is around; and as it happens, I have unfinished matters with him that I have to discuss first. But please be prepared to come and meet me at short notice'.

The staff members left, studiously avoiding looking at the stranger. They went in a rather good frame of mind, in the belief that the stranger's narration had not made them suspects themselves - in some way or other - in the director's eyes. Sujata watched them go with a wry face and then turned to her ace operator.

She still carefully refrained from calling him by name. 'Well, I think your happy buccaneer days here are over now that your identity stands exposed. But I still need vital information from you. When is the next "Satanic" meeting taking place?'

'Certainly Dr. Sujata, I will let you know as soon as I find out. I have a feeling it will be soon now'.

'Not too soon, I hope. I have to be away to Delhi for a few days, for meetings at the Human Resources Ministry. But you can call me; Bhaskaran will connect you on a safe line'.

She looked the man straight in the face. 'And, use any method you have to, to get this information: phone tapping, whatever. You said that you have all the clearances'.

# XXIII

A few days after her return from the meeting with the 'higher authorities', Sujata was coming down the front steps to her car to go to another meeting, this time at the Calicut Management Association. She was half-way down steps when she heard Bhaskaran calling out after her.

'Madam, it's your call on the secure line'.

Sujata looked up and seeing Bhaskaran running down the steps to help her, ran up, past the secretary, and through the lobby into her room. Bhaskaran looked after her in silent admiration. So agile, madam, he thought; must be doing treadmills in her bungalow.

'So, do you have the information?', Sujata asked straightaway.

'Yes. At 10 AM on Saturday'.

Not good, Sujata thought. A holiday for IIMK, people tend not to keep time.

'And the location?'

'Your guess was perfect', Dr. Sujata. She imagined she could see him smiling.

Sujata put the phone down at once, not bothering to

say thank you or goodbye, and immediately called Jose. He must have sensed the urgency in her voice, for he came running in without knocking–just like he did when reporting on the absconding pedophile, Rubin.

'Jose. Listen carefully. This is a life and death matter. You do this: call Mohan and tell him to be here at sharp 9.15 AM on Saturday'. She paused, thinking.

'No, not here in my office, but at the smaller conference room where we sometimes conduct faculty and staff interviews. Tell him only I and an official from the Human Resources Ministry will be there for the meeting'.

Jose nodded, taking notes, but wondering why a ministry official would want to meet Mohan, rather than the two faculty members who were on the board of directors.

'Also, Jose, ask Ravindran to keep Mohan in the conference room under the pretext that I and the official will be arriving there after a private meeting at the guesthouse.

'Ravindran, madam? But I am here, I could do it'.

'No. Jose, you are coming with me, as will be Bhaskaran. I mean, on Saturday morning'.

'Where to. Madam? Exactly at 9.15?'

Always a stickler for time and exact location to 10 meters radius accuracy, Sujata sighed. A little more flexibility would have been welcome. Yet, the qualities that seemed tiresome in Jose's makeup were also the ones that made him a rock-solid, totally dependable deputy.

'Well, not exactly at 9.15, perhaps, but be prepared to leave then', Sujata said. 'Just be informed that the three of us have something very important to do on Saturday morning. We have to be prepared to be innovative, even with respect to time and places. Is that enough to go on for you now?

'Yes, madam!'. One could almost hear the clicking of Jose's heels, military-style.

'And at 9.45, Ravindran will inform Mohan that the official had been held up: let's say, due to some important calls from the Ministry. And, that the meeting has been canceled, that it may be rescheduled to the middle of next week'.

Strange orders, but Jose was not confused. Rather, the adrenalin was flowing richly in his veins, for he had a feeling that some real action was being plotted by Sujata, something inconceivable from the earlier directors.

'I understand Sujata madam, perfectly. Mohan will be at the conference from 9.15 to 9.45, and then he is free to go to Timbuktu if he wants to'.

'Yes, Timbuktu, if he wants to. But I have a feeling that he will run straight into us before that'.

'Us? Where?'

Sujata sighed again. It was not easy to satisfy Jose. She did not answer his query but nodded at him as a sign that their planning meeting was over.


When informed of the tripartite meeting on Saturday, Mohan sat pondering over his significance. Not in the director's room, but at the conference room where formal interviews are usually held; a Ministry official taking part, probably a member of the Board of Directors. A dormant hope was rekindled in Mohan: this could mean only one thing, that his demand to be placed in the faculty cadre at the associate professor level was finally being taken up. The informal arrangement with no pre-announced interview plan was understandable: such a change in cadre-type is not standard practice, being considered case by case only. In fact, the only case known to Mohan was that of the IIMK librarian being placed at the associate professor level after finishing a Ph.D.

On Saturday morning, the to-be-faculty systems manager took special care with his appearance. He plumped for a light brown safari suit that accentuated his pallid complexion, which, together with the crooked smile that he practiced in front of the mirror, would have given a sensitive person sleepless nights.

When Mohan took his seat in the conference room, it lay desolate. But he was happy to note that three plates with cashew nut packets in them had been placed on the table with mineral water bottles by their side. He knew that visiting dignitaries and officials had a weakness for Kerala cashews, export quality. He settled down to wait, practicing his self-introduction which may be required when the proceedings began.

He was unaware that as soon as he entered the office lobby, Jose had rung up Sujata. She laid out the day's action plan at once.

'Let Ravindran take him to the conference room at precisely 9.15, make him feel that things are moving on schedule. You come along now to join me, bring Bhaskaran along'.

At 9.15, just when Mohan was entering the conference room, the doorbell rang at Sekhar's house. He hesitated. Who could it be now? Perhaps a child student of the dance classes next door, who had finally come for the chocolates that he promised? That thought raised some wicked thoughts in his mind, and he quickly opened the front door, not even bothering to use the peephole.

When Sekhar opened the door, he could see no one at first. Then, Sujata, who had been standing away from the line of vision of the peephole, stepped out in front of him. Behind her stood Jose and Bhaskaran.

The blood drained from Sekhar's face, and he clutched at the porch railing for support, to steady himself.

'Nice place you have here, Sekhar', Sujata said, standing in the porch and looking around. 'And, that house there is the dance teacher's, I understand. Lovely children, her students, aren't they? You love children too, I understand, but in which manner?'

Sekhar tried to say something, but only inaudible sounds escaped his mouth.

'So, you have a bachelor's accommodation on campus, and then this bungalow: a well-kept secret too, since you claim no rent allowance for this. So, this house address does not enter the institute records'.

No time to waste, Sujata told herself as Sekhar still tottered on weak legs trying to find something to say. She glanced meaningfully at Bhaskaran, who, interpreting her order, pushed Sekhar roughly through the door into the living room.

'Expecting your partner-in-crime weren't you, Sujata asked as Bhaskaran deposited the man in an easy chair against a wall, out of bounds for windows.

Sekhar's mind must have been working quickly, for he smiled weakly at everyone assembled in the room and said in an innocent voice,

'Madam, yes, indeed, I had rented this house and did not want IIMK to bear the cost as I am using it only as an art studio, not as a dwelling'. He waved a hand at the paintings on the wall. 'Some are my work'.

'And where maybe the dirty films and videos?, Sujata was brutally frank. 'Sekhar, don't waste your breath. The game is up. Your housekeeper is not to be seen today, isn't it so? She is in the hands of some very capable, rough, and tough policewomen who are interrogating her right now. She has already spilled the beans, nothing sordid left unsaid. Besides, my agent, the ace operator you met last week, had struck up a hot romance with her, and she has told him everything too. She was planning to elope with him, leaving this evil house as she put it'.

Sekhar was no fool.  In fact, he was at the cutting edge of research in his management field. He could see that the game was indeed up and took an instant decision to cooperate in the investigation that seemed to have been launched with all the guns blazing.

'Madam, I can see that we cannot bluff you. All the rooms upstairs, except the hall which has some paintings, contain what you are looking for.  But believe me madam Sujata, Mohan took the decisions. I could not utter a word against him'.

'We'll find out about the depth and willingness of your engagement in this horrible crime', Sujata said ominously and then looked at her watch. 'Your friend will be here soon. You will do exactly as I say'.

She looked around the living room and then went into

the adjoining rooms. One was the large master bedroom downstairs, and the other was a smaller office room, but with a pull-out sofa bed as well. While she was exploring the rooms Bhaskaran stood with folded arms in front of Sekhar, like a sentinel.

"You will do exactly as I say', Sujata repeated when she came back to the living room. 'We will leave you here now but will be in those rooms, watching every move you make, listening to every word that you say. You will admit Mohan when he rings the bell and behave naturally. Let him do all the talking. Prompt him to talk more on what he has done and what he plans to do'.

'Get him to talk more on what?', Sekhar asked, finding his voice.

'Do I have to tell you? Get him to talk on your links with local and international paedophile gangs, about your plans to get rid of Divya'.

Sekhar sat up in shock on hearing Divya's name mentioned. He tried to say something, probably by way of denial, but the words didn't come out.

'So, we are going into the other rooms now. Do exactly as I told you: it will do you some good when you stand in the dock'.

Sujata and Bhaskaran went into the large bedroom while Jose disappeared behind the door of the office room. Sekhar did not look in their directions, sat perfectly still, eyes fixed on the front door.

The doorbell rang after about ten minutes. Twice, thrice, long rings before Sekhar could reach the door.

'Are you deaf or something? I rang several times'.

Mohan pushed past his partner into the room and threw himself down on the large sofa in front of the twin windows.

'So, what was it about?', Sekhar tried to keep his voice steady. 'The meeting, I mean'.

Mohan glared at him. 'You look nervous. Don't worry, Rubin has left. I think he believed someone recognized him, but he has not given us away: a true professional'.

'Then we are safe, things can go on as usual', Sekhar said, not daring to look Mohan in the face.

'Yes, but we still have to move our hardware and software and all the videos. I am arranging transport for next weekend. This place is too close to IIMK. It was ok till that interfering do-gooder of a girl started coming here, to the neighbouring house. The dancer and that friend of hers, Roshan, had never even looked in this direction, ever'.

'Divya is a curious person by nature, too curious, wouldn't you say?', Sekhar said, throwing a glance at the bedroom.

The glance had not escaped Mohan's eyes. 'Why are the curtains drawn? Have you been screwing the housekeeper in there?', he asked, guffawing, despite the sore mood he was in.

Sekhar quickly changed the subject. 'Do you think Divya would disclose what she had heard from the housekeeper? I mean, when she has recovered'.

Mohan was looking again at the drawn curtains, frowning, but he responded. 'No, I am pretty sure she will not. She wouldn't want to destroy Rakesh's life even though her bloody heart will bleed for the children. She will just stop coming to this hated corner of the world. That is what we wanted, right?'

He paused, thinking. 'But I wonder about the housekeeper'.

'I heard you asking about the housekeeper earlier also', Sujata said, emerging from the bedroom. 'How good of you be concerned about her! Not many think of the welfare of women in the informal sector'.

Mohan jumped up from the sofa, staring at Sujata as though he has seen a ghost, in total shock and bewilderment. But then, his brain churning at full speed, he managed to bring a pleased expression on to his face.

'Madam, were you here? Oh, Sekhar invited you too! How nice, he kept it as a surprise for me. It has become an informal housewarming party for his bungalow'.

'Shut up you devil, you child molester', Sujata said brutally. 'We know everything. The housekeeper is in police custody, being interrogated by the best, the toughest policewomen. She has already spilled the beans completely, hoping for clemency. After all, it's not her set-up, it's yours. She has been only an instrument'.

Sujata motioned to Bhaskaran, who was standing guarding the front exit. He took Mohan firmly by his upper arm and deposited him in a chair right next to Sekhar.

'Are you willing to talk now?', Sujata asked holding Mohan's eyes with her own. He had given up the playacting and was now sitting erect with an inscrutable expression on his face, deathly pale.

I am going to wipe that expression off your dirty face, Sujata thought but said civilly enough: 'Start by telling us why you brought Rakesh into the plot. I think I know why, but want to hear it from the master-plotter, from the horse's mouth'.

Suddenly, Jose broke in. He just couldn't contain himself. 'But, madam, what is this being said about Dr. Rakesh? That he has done something terrible? I won't believe such malignant tales".

'You answer Jose', Sujata said, looking at Mohan. But he still sat with an impassive face that seemed to convey contempt for the trial being held.

Now it was Sujata who couldn't control herself. She strode up to Mohan and hit him hard across the face, on the left cheek. His face ricocheted on impact to the right, but then he straightened his face and resumed his statue-like bearing. However, he was now looking directly at Sujata, and hatred blazed from his eyes.

'Oh, would you glare at Madam like that?', Bhaskaran shouted, and rushing to Mohan, dealt him a heavy blow, right on the face again. Mohan fell off the chair and lay on the floor, bleeding from a cut on his lips. Bhaskaran pulled him up, raising a fist again.

'No, Bhaskaran, no more', Sujata said sternly. 'If you hit him again with your BSF muscles, you'll kill him'.

Bhaskaran lifted Mohan easily and threw him back on to the chair, next to his partner who shrank away deep into his easy chair, as if trying to roll himself up into a ball for self-protection.

'I am sorry that I didn't enlighten you sufficiently at the office, Jose; I mean, the other day when the ace operator had clarified a few things. There was no time then for explanations, only for action–and for making plans for action. Besides, Jose, believe it or not, IIMK walls have ears!'.

Sujata signaled to Bhaskaran to take up a position directly in front of the pedophiles in custody. Then she turned to Jose again.

'Jose, don't you worry, Rakesh is not at all a part of this paedophile group. The housekeeper was told by Sekhar to mention Rakesh's name to Divya, as being the IIMK professor who regularly comes for the child-porn sessions and activities. In fact, Rakesh was invited by Sekhar once to see the paintings displayed here–and some in the hall above. That was the day the housekeeper tricked Divya and told her that Rakesh was there right then. Divya saw Rakesh through a window–and her world collapsed'.

All of a sudden, a nightingale broke out in song, tuning into full volume right away. Sujata paused to listen. Then she noticed Bhaskaran, who had tilted his head to one side, listening in ecstasy to the melody.

'No, no, Bhaskaran, this won't do', she called out sharply. 'Keep your eyes on those two. They are more dangerous than you can imagine. You can listen to the nightingale later from the dance teacher's house, I'm sure'.

Bhaskaran snapped into attention, glaring balefully at the criminals as if to say, 'don't try any funny stuff with me now!'. Sekhar cowered backwards into his chair at the fierce expression on the secretary's face, but Mohan sat rigid like a sphinx. Blood from his cut lips dropped down, staining the collar of the safari suit: he had not even bothered to wipe his mouth.

'So the housekeeper has narrated all this to the police',

Jose reflected loudly.

'Yes, but I was informed of all this by my man, the ace operator'. Sujata still studiously avoided mentioning the agent's name. 'You see, he struck up a romance with the housekeeper, courted her with valuable gifts, even a gold necklace, I believe–which I will not refund as the cost of his operations! Anyhow, he has helped me partly in the capacity of a friend, so it has not been a purely professional, commercial relationship'.

'I gathered as much', Jose smiled, 'the way he was sprawling out in madam's office sofa, I thought: this man is a friend of madam, not a paid agent'.

'Both, as a matter of fact: you cannot demand people's time without some compensation. That is management wisdom. As I was saying, the housekeeper told him everything she knew about what the house was being used for. It turned out to be really valuable information: the woman was a keen and curious observer. I think this criminal duo had not reckoned with her being such a busybody'.

'One more doubt, Dr. Sujata', Jose blurted  out, eager not to miss out any piece fitted together in the puzzle. 'We know that a car almost ran over Divya, a deliberate attempt on her life. I thought that the hypothesis was that a shadowy drug mafia group with links inside IIMK was responsible for the attempt'.

'Well….', Sujata said doubtfully. 'I don't know if we ever held that hypothesis seriously. Besides, as we heard from Elizabeth, the girl Divya thought to be under the influence of drugs was only staggering about lacking her lenses'.

'But the attempt to run Divya over with the car?'

'Oh, that. I forgot to tell you. The ace agent witnessed the incident. He said it was clear that it was not an attempt on her life: the driver turned the car away sharply well before reaching her. It was a ploy to frighten her, for a definite reason'.

Sujata turned to Mohan. 'I guess you thought the roar of that car would be enough to frighten Divya into not coming anywhere near your porn palace. The idea was also, presumably, that she would relate the attempt to her repeated indiscretion in 'spying upon' the drug-addicted girl student'.

Perhaps feeling left out, Bhaskaran shifted his position a little to face Sujata sideways and said: 'I always had my doubt about this fellow Mohan; thought he was rotten inside, morally'.

Bunkum, Sujata said to herself. Bhaskaran probably never gave a second thought to Mohan. He had more important things to think of, such as disposing of his excess-quota ex-army rum. But she said aloud:

'Of course, Bhaskaran, you have a highly developed sixth sense: must be due to all that prowling around in the dark at the borders'.

Bhaskaran straightened his back a little more, proudly.

Sujata looked at her watch. 'Believe it or not, Jose, I do have a meeting with a Ministry official, though not the one Mr. Mohan was hoping to attend and present his credentials. So, I have to leave now. And, Bhaskaran, stay alert now, don't take your eyes off them'.

'I am fully alert madam', Bhaskaran said, and to prove

his point, suddenly dropped on to the floor and started doing one-arm pushups, still keeping his eyes on the two men in front.

'Oh, cut it out', Sujata cried out sharply. 'Get up, back to your position. Just make sure that the lullaby of that bird does not put you to sleep standing up'.

She saw Jose looking at her, awaiting further instructions. 'Jose, you stay here with Bhaskaran. A team will be here soon to pick these men up. Oh, yes, and you were asking me the other day about the lack of evidence against Rubin. I am sure that the interrogation of these two sadists will throw up enough evidence to nail him as well'.

Sujata stepped out on to the porch and on to the narrow driveway, in reality just a footpath. She turned to look at the house once more. 'A house of evil', the words echoed in her mind again. 'But this pleasant, tranquil countryside will soon claim it rightfully back into its fold'.

On an impulse, she veered away to the left, stepping gingerly between flowerpots, thinking she could get a glimpse of the Melody King. But the nightingale continued singing, supremely at home in its familiar surroundings, blissfully undetected and undisturbed amongst  the thick foliage of the mango tree.

# Epilogue

Roshan found Rakesh at a table at the far corner of the dining hall on the second floor, on the narrow glass corridor jutting out towards the hills.

'I came as soon as I got your message', he said, 'it sounded urgent'.

'Not really', Rakesh said, patting the chair next to him. 'Sit down. I'll order some coffee. I just thought we should have a chat since you leave tomorrow for your summer internship'.

He waved towards the distant hills. 'You will miss this. I wish this glass corridor was like a fire-force ladder that I could use to zoom in towards those Wayanad mountains'.

Roshan laughed. 'You'll save a lot of time. It's one and a half hours there by road!'

Rajesh turned around to look intently at him. 'But what's this I hear, that you may not complete the programme? Can't your start-up wait till that?'

'I would like to, Dr. Rakesh, but my project partner, my classmate in the U.S, with whom I have my internship, actually a partnership, is rearing to go. His investment funds have maturedand he doesn't want to keep them liquid. Besides, the degree certificate is not important for me - I feel that I have acquired the know-how needed to run my own business'.

Rakesh shrugged. 'Well, you know best.  And it is good to

see students valuing the knowledge gained more than the degree certificate. But, a project on windmills: what made you choose it?'

'My partner liked it, thought it was the best bet for his return on investment - but so did I.  I always had this thing, a fascination for windmills, ever since I read Don Quixote as a boy'.

'Good', Rakesh said approvingly. 'I always hold the view that you should hold on, if possible, live out, your childhood fantasies. Also, the government will pay you handsomely for the renewable energy generated from an inexhaustible source'.

They sat in silence for a while, sipping their coffee.

'You'll miss this green campus', Rakesh mused; gazing out.

'Yes, but I'm back after the summer - should be here for the first term of the second year before leaving. I have heard this may be the most scenic of all IIM campuses. We all have to be grateful to Dr. Sujata for getting rid of the ugly, inhuman elements. Really intriguing, how she could it all alone'.

'I think she came well-prepared, Roshan because she was forewarned about how difficult this place could be. So, she set up an information system even before she landed up here, had trustworthy agents in place'

'But the drug mafia turned out to be a false alarm, isn't it?'

'No, I wouldn't say that at all. Links to the drug syndicate exists here, but they are inactive because they have realized that Dr. Sujata is a formidable adversary. So, in her initial concern about the syndicate, she was not being Don Quixote-like, was not "tilting at the windmills" as the saying goes. The drug mafia is no imaginary enemy like Don Quixote's windmills'.

'That is disturbing', Roshan said, a worried frown on his face. 'So these other ugly elements are just waiting for the term of the "Iron Lady" to be over'.

'That's right: only a brief term of five years. The syndicate which has its tentacles in every academic institution, has all the time in the world. They are biding their time, waiting in the wings, for her exit. They expect that future directors, like past ones, would be more lackadaisical. Dr. Sujata is an aberration for them'.

Rakesh turned sideways to look Roshan directly in the eyes. 'But, to come to more personal matters, Roshan, tell me, will you not miss some people terribly when you leave? You will, of course, see Diya when she rejoins IIMK next term, i.e., the first term of the next academic year. You will miss Shalini too, I am sure'.

Roshan glanced at Rakesh quickly and then averted his eyes.

'You know, Roshan, I was having a conversation with Divya precisely on this subject: about your equation with Shalini. She told me that once she cleverly drew out Shakini, asking her if she was much older than you. Shalini replied that the age difference was four years when it is actually 4.9 years. So, she conveniently rounded off the difference to the nearest downside whole number, which lay more distant than the upper whole number. Now, to me that is significant!'.

Roshan said in a low voice. "Frankly, Dr. Rakesh, I feel it is time for me to reveal what is on my mind to her, ask her to be my partner'.

'Partner? In the windmill project?'

Roshan smiled. 'Well, maybe that too. But I was using the term in a larger sense. Maybe I'll have this conversation with her when I return after the summer internship'.

'I am surprised, Roshan. You, who claim to hate procrastination, dilly-dallying, putting off the most major step in your life right now'.

Rakesh turned to look down at the garden below. 'It is a fine day out there now, the best of Calicut. Why delay, take the chance on her today'.

Roshan followed his eyes. A fine day out there as he said.

Pale, mellow sunlight flooding the green campus, giving it almost a yellowish hue.

Perhaps an auspicious day in her eyes, in her professional terminology.

www.ingramcontent.com/pod-product-compliance
Lightning Source LLC
LaVergne TN
LVHW041505170726
843492LV00005B/1379